Four
on the
EDGE

by Heidi Borrink

Pacific Press Publishing Association
Boise, Idaho
Oshawa, Ontario, Canada

Edited by Marvin Moore
Designed by Dennis Ferree
Cover photos by Stan Sinclair
Typeset in 10/12 Bookman

Library of Congress Cataloging-in-Publication Data:
Borrink, Heidi, 1965-
  Four on the edge: they sought freedom and ac-
ceptance, they found something else / Heidi Borrink.
        p.   cm.
  Summary: Presents the interrelated stories of
four teenagers by revealing their thoughts as they
make choices about drugs, sex, abortion, and God.
  ISBN 0-8163-1053-X
  1. Christian life. [1. Conduct of life.]
  I. Title
PZ7.B648495Fo   1992   91-3073
[Fic]—dc20   •   CIP
                                           AC

91 92 93 94 95 • 5 4 3 2 1

1

Jim

I get the same highs almost every morning when I go to school. These are pretty much sure things that I know I can count on:

My football jacket.

My car (even though it's a tank).

Holly meeting me at my locker with a kiss for me, looking all snuggly in one of those fluffy sweaters of hers.

Oh, I forgot. My smokes! One smoke in the parking lot is just fine. Then there are some of the guys from the football team slapping each other around before first period. The best is on the day of the game. There'll be banners up and posters on our lockers. OK, so maybe the posters aren't the biggest turn-on. It's the cheerleaders in their flippy little skirts and nice smooth legs that I like. Man! Holly always looks so perfect. Maybe she *is* perfect. And she knows she's the luckiest girl in the school to have me.

Whoa, listen to me! Yeah, right, big man on campus.

If I wasn't a football player, what would I be? Some kind of bum, probably. A stoner, maybe, or a brain. Or maybe one of those theater types. Uh-huh. Maybe I wouldn't have Holly if I wasn't on the team. I dunno, sometimes I think people expect too much from me. Like I have this image I have to keep up. It's one thing to be the wide receiver for the team. It's another thing to feel like everyone is watching you or expecting you to act a certain way.

It seems like I'm supposed to have this big LEADER sign on. Star wide receiver and Christian dynamo all wrapped up into one great fella. Why does it all have to matter so much? Just because I've been to every youth group outing, Bible study conference, and ice-cream social doesn't mean I'm all together and all excited about keeping all the rules. For once I'd like to do what I want to do.

There's this kid in my humanities class named Keeler. I never noticed him until we got put together in groups for our final projects. I hate these group things. One person always has the ideas and does all the work. The rest just kind of blow it off, copy the outlines, and snow the teacher with something profound when they're supposed to. No one really gets into it. I can already tell it's going to be a real swell combination of people. There's me and Holly, who already seems to be doing her spiritual leader thing, and then there's this quiet guy and this airy girl who doesn't understand what's going on, and then Keeler. Keeler's cool. I can tell he's really smart or something, like he knows what he wants to say, yet at the same time he doesn't give a rip. What I mean is, he doesn't care what people think of him. He slumps at his desk with this bulldog glare on his face. I notice he wears an earring. I used to think that was for fags, but I think that's just the way he dresses. He wears all these old clothes, like old blazers and sweaters and these goofy old men's shoes.

We're sitting there trying to figure out what Mr. Cardigan (that's his name, it really is) is telling us, and Keeler's making these jokes under his breath. He mumbles, "Mr. Cardigan Sweater. Oh, this is just the niftiest assignment. . . . Boys and girls, now make sure you all work together . . ." No one hears him but me. He's pretty funny. Anyway, like I said, we had this group thing to do.

"So what's the deal here?" Keeler says.

Holly tries hard to ignore him. She explains the assignment to everyone like she's a stewardess or something. "How are we going to do this? I think the best way would be to present the two arguments."

The topic is natural law. Free will versus determinism. Right away, Holly digs up an example of determinism by using the Bible. She really makes me squirm when she gets that lofty look somewhere between her eyes and her nostrils. Give me a break.

"Why don't we use Daniel as an example of how God used an individual to accomplish His plan to change society? That's what determinism really is, isn't it? God knows how things are supposed to happen, like it's already decided. God decided He would use Daniel . . ."

She gets all excited about issues and picking sides. Sometimes I really admire her for that, but right now it really bugs me. I can tell it bugs Keeler too because right away he says, "Wait a minute. Daniel didn't have to do anything. He acted according to what he decided to do. Just because God used him to impact on society doesn't necessarily mean Daniel agreed. People aren't puppets. They have a choice, you know. What if Daniel had made another decision? Then would God have picked someone else?"

I notice Holly is getting flustered. He really shut her up. I feel trapped, like I don't want my girlfriend to look stupid, yet I want Keeler to like me. I thought what he said had some truth in it. Holly always seems to think she's right, or that there's only one way to look at things. When someone speaks an opposing opinion, she can't handle it.

Holly blurts, "Without his faith, Daniel would've failed."

Keeler shifts a little in his chair and stares blankly at Holly. Holly is shooting these looks at me that say, "Rescue me, Jim!" I want to get into this discussion, I really do. Keeler has raised some good points. I don't know why Holly has to turn arguments like this into such a challenge of wills. It's only a class, or a grade. She gets all on her haunches, like, "I dare you to oppose me."

I don't know what makes my mouth say this, but I say, "How can you prove that?"

"What?" Holly asks.

"How can you prove that Daniel would've failed God's plan if he didn't have his strength or faith or whatever?"

"That's the point—we don't know."

Swell. That makes Holly real pleased. I'm on Keeler's side now, she thinks. If only she knew that I don't exactly know what this discussion is all about and I would like this class to end so that the tension in the air would blow over . . .

This girl Becky says, "Why don't we just have a debate? Jim, you and Keeler seem to agree on the free-will side; you two would make a good team."

So that's how it ends up. Holly gets paired up with the shy guy. Keeler is smirking. I'm not sure I want to work with him.

"I'm sure your girlfriend's embarrassed. Real perky now," Keeler says under his breath.

"She'll get over it," I say. "Do you understand this stuff?"

"Oh yeah. It's real simple. I'll explain it to you. When do you want to get together and work on it?" he says.

"Man, I dunno. I've got a big game tomorrow night. After that I should be able to concentrate on this thing." He must think I'm a big jockhead now.

"OK. Whatever," he says.

After class I try and catch up with Holly, who

is moving through the halls like a ball of fire. She's ticked off now, I can tell.

"Hey, what's your problem?" I say. "Are you mad that I'm not on your team?"

"I cannot stand that Keeler guy. He thinks he knows—I'm sure he just wanted to make me look like a total fool," she says.

"Yeah, right. Don't you know anything about philosophy? That's what it's all about—taking a position and defending it, looking at it analytically or something. You're just getting all emotional about it when it's just an assignment. It's not supposed to get you upset. Maybe what you were trying to prove is just as valid as what Keeler and I were defending. Hey, what do I know? I was just faking it."

"Then why did you end up on Keeler's team?"

"Because . . . I don't know, because he's a smart guy. Who cares?"

I can usually get Holly out of her moods. I can't stand them for very long. I tease her, "Your face is red hot, babe. I love it when your lips get all pouty."

"Stop!" she whines, laughing.

I know she loves me. She'll be bouncing up and down on the sidelines tomorrow night.

CHAPTER

Keeler

I don't know how I ended up going to the football game anyway. I mean, I don't cheer. I don't even know the rules of the game or what's happening on the field half the time. I don't know anyone on the team, really, except for that Jim Peterson in humanities and this guy Dwayne from shop class. He's all right. I didn't have anyone who I particularly cared to go with tonight. I just showed up.

This isn't my school, I keep telling myself. I just transferred here when we moved. It's real swell when it's your senior year. Like, I really want new friends for one year. It will be over soon. My parents made me go here. They thought it would be an easier adjustment for me in a private *Christian* school. Everyone would be friendly, and there wouldn't be as many unknowns to worry about like drugs and sex and gangs like there would be in a public school. Well, guess what? There are

11

the same kinds of things here, Mom and Dad, only on a sneakier and intensified level. If a girl's a slut, then she's the slut of the whole school. If a guy like me's a rich kid with a car, weird clothes, and an earring, then he's the radical of the school. And the cycle gets smaller and smaller. Everyone talks, and the little groups of people are obvious. Shoot, the school only has 700 kids. And they all go to the same churches and know each other's families and stuff.

That's why I came to the game stoned. It's kind of nice, actually. I can say I participated in the school spirit, showed my face, but I can be detached from the entire event. It's not a big deal, being alone in a cheering crowd, chanting cheers with the pep club. At least my parents think I'm fitting in and getting involved. That's good, because maybe then my stepmother will shut up about my attitude and get off my back about being unfriendly and bitter. Yes, I'm bitter. I fit in pretty well when I was at Ridgeview. If my parents would've put it on hold one more year, I would've maybe graduated with a handful of friends and some awards or something.

I can't give you much of a play-by-play on the game, but I do remember the ending. Jim ran down the field and caught this incredible pass in this diving catch. I wish I could run like that. Just to run and run with the ball in my hands. Touchdown! And the crowd roars, stomps, and screams, and the game's over. I ran hard and nobody caught me and I won the game for our team. Wow, what finesse.

After the game was over, I walked out near

the sidelines. I didn't think I would go up to the team members and slap them on their rear ends and say, "Hey, man, awesome game, good game, man . . ." But I kind of wanted to see Jim. I just sort of wanted him to know that I came to the game. I passed by the team members. They were pouring buckets all over each other. Jim spotted me. He was heading toward the locker room dangling his helmet. I heard myself say, "Hey, man, great game. Close game. Was that fumble in the fourth quarter planned or what?"

"No, but going long on first down was," Jim said.

Yeah, like, *I'm the big football fan!* After that I didn't know what to say. I just stood there feeling like a squirrel. I wanted to see what he'd say next. He had to get changed or get on the bus or something. I fumbled with my keys like I had somewhere to go.

"So do you want to get together tomorrow and do some, uh, free will and determinism?" I said.

"Yeah, I guess we should. Do you wanna just meet at Red Rooster restaurant after church sometime?"

"Sure, yeah, that would be great. How about at two?"

He agreed and ran off to the bus that was waiting for him. I drove around for about an hour, smoked some more, and went to bed.

CHAPTER

3

Holly

This night would've been so totally perfect if I hadn't been such a priss and freaked out in the car. I swear, Jim must think I'm psycho now.

We had so much fun tonight. I love October nights. They're so spooky. That moldy smell of dead leaves and the first chill and damp raw in the air. And the moon was really bright tonight. I think it was a harvest moon or something 'cause it was like yellowish orange and really bright.

I went with Jim on the hayride tonight with our youth group. Hayrides are kind of silly. All you really do is ride around in a field on the back of a wagon, throw hay and throw more hay. I wasn't really into it, so I sat down right there in the hay and waited for Jim to see me. I think I just wanted to roll in the hay or have him bury me in the stuff. My mother would kill me because I'm like really allergic to hay or dust or something and I always get sick after these things, but I didn't care. I just

14

wanted to forget all the stupid freshmen guys on our wagon and pull Jim over me and cover us all over with hay.

I pulled the leg of Jim's jeans and then grabbed his leg. He fell right on my lap. I guess I didn't think he'd react, but he started grabbing handfuls of hay and straw and stuffing them down my jacket. I was screaming and shoving hay at his face and in his hair. Then he started tickling me, and I didn't know where I was in the hay. I'm sure I looked terrible. My eyes were itching like crazy. The ride was over, and we had some hot cider in Mr. Watts's barn and sang some songs.

I love it when Jim is playful. He's so cute. I felt so guilty because I just couldn't wait to leave. I wanted to be with Jim. Just us in his car. Even though he didn't kiss me or anything on the hayride, I could feel his breath on my face, his warm face brushing my cold cheeks. I like Jim for how strong he is, crushing the laughter out of me until I could hardly breathe. I just couldn't wait to be in the car with him by ourselves.

When we left the hayride, I could tell in the car that Jim had been thinking the same thing. He was in a snugly mood. I slid over on the car seat next to him and started kissing his neck. I was really brave or something. He tried starting the car. Then he stopped and shut off the motor. He told me to stop.

"Can we at least wait until we get out of the driveway here so the whole youth group and Coach Barnes don't see us?" He laughed and looked at me in a way that made me kind of giddy and excited. I didn't know quite what he had in mind, but I couldn't wait to find out.

I'm lucky my house has a long driveway. The driveway kind of begins at the edge of some woods, and you can't see the entrance from the house, which is nice when your boyfriend is bringing you home and you want to make out for an hour or two. Jim usually turns the engine off and then hits the lights so that my parents don't wake up and wait for me or anything queer like that.

When we get to my house, my heart is pounding. I'm so excited. I really don't have to do much. I just give him these little kisses and he does the rest. Tonight was the first time I felt like I could totally give him all of me. We were kissing, and I couldn't breathe. Everything was happening so fast. He reached over to lower the bucket seat flat.

It was like an alarm went off in my head. "Danger! Danger!" I thought.

I felt his hands tangle in my hair, then touch my sweater. Uh-oh, that's a little too . . . oh, no. I hear all the youth group talks on *how far is too far?* My mouth hurts. I push him away a little. I want him. I like this, but we can't. We shouldn't. Oh, no, I never thought—is this it? Is this how it happens?

Suddenly, this breathless voice that sounds like mine stops him somewhere on my neck. "Jim, wait a minute . . . we can't do this. I mean, I can't have sex with you. Not now, OK?" I want to cry, because all this feels so wonderful and I want more and more and I don't want him to be mad, but we just can't.

Jim sits up straight. He looks like a small animal. His brown eyes are so gentle, like a baby deer's. In this quiet voice he says, "I'm sorry. I'm sorry . . . I thought you . . . I didn't realize there was anything wrong . . ."

Now I feel all pristine and scared. "Wrong?" My voice trembles. I look up at Jim and can't meet his eyes. "It feels so good, Jim. My feelings tell me it's all right, but my head says it's wrong. I love you so much . . . please believe me . . . I . . . I just don't know what we're doing. I don't want us to ruin it. Can you just hold me for a while?"

Jim doesn't say anything. He waits. He just sits there, kind of injured or tired. Then he says, "No, I can't just hold you for a while. I know what you mean. I grew up knowing the same things. And if I hold you for a while . . . you know, maybe you, uh, maybe we'd be, you know, sorry."

I can tell Jim's a little upset with me, even though he seems to agree. It feels like he has left me alone in the car, the steamy car in the dark of the driveway.

"I better go, huh?" I whisper.

"Yeah, it's probably late."

"I really love you, Jim."

"I know. I . . . uh . . . I love you too," he says.

I get out of the car and walk all the way up the driveway in the dark. I feel like I have lost *him* and lost part of *me*. I wonder if we'll ever get that close again. I wonder when he says that he loves me if that means he loves me even if we can't have sex.

CHAPTER

Sonia

Holly says I should start trying different things with my hair or start wearing some makeup or something. I guess I never really thought I needed it. There's not much I can do with my hair; it's so short now. I got it cut really short, like a crew cut, and the barber shaved it all up the back, so it's all velvety like kitten fur. I love it. I took extra time getting ready this morning, the one time I really worked at looking good. I don't know, Holly makes me feel like I'm a guy or something. Maybe I should try looking sexier or whatever I'm supposed to look like to get a boyfriend.

Holly never has to work at looking good. She's just naturally beautiful. She knows it too. She's got the money for sweaters and designer jeans and shoes. I can't remember her any other way. And she always smells delicious. These are all the things that Jim must love

18

about her. She's so lucky and he's so lucky. They just look good together. The popular senior couple. I'm the one who feels like the little girl, like the kid sister who hasn't discovered boys yet. My mom says I don't need to worry about dating; then she tells me I should act more like a lady and dress more feminine so that the boys will like me. She was real thrilled with my hair. She said I had the same kind of haircut Dad had the first time she met him when he was in the service. Gee, that's handsome. Hey, I don't care. At least I like it. But what if they're right and I never get noticed because I'm not pretty or cutsie enough?

So this morning I was spiking my bangs up with this thick new gel I just bought. I love it. It's like glue. It makes my hair stand right up; then I spray it so that it's all stiff and bonded. I wasn't ready yet when Jim began honking the horn in the driveway. He's such a jerk. I was going to try some eyeliner and maybe outline my lips like Holly told me. She said the eyeliner would help my eyes look bigger and bluer. She said I have great lips, which would look fuller with some lipstick. So my hair looked good and I wore my new cream sweater, but I was mad I didn't get time to try the makeup out.

Jim was already in the car with the radio blasting. "Thanks a lot, loser. We're not *that* late—what's the big deal?"

"Just hurry up, OK? I said I'd pick up this kid Keeler. He lives a couple blocks over from us. I just met him. He's pretty cool. What's wrong with getting to school early?"

Nothing may be wrong for Jim, but I hate being early. I don't like to stand around and wait in the halls for the first person I know to come along. I don't like standing around watching for a familiar face to appear in the bus loads of kids streaming in the front door. The only days I like are when there's a game and I can put up posters and hang out with Holly and the cheerleaders and get excused from first period.

I'm starting to resent Jim. He could be in trouble so easily if it wasn't for me. He trusts me not to tell Mom and Dad he smokes. He used to smoke in the car while we rode to school. That made me really sick, and I never said anything until one day a couple weeks ago I told him his smoking was disgusting and that if he wanted me to keep quiet about his stupid habit he'd better wait until I was out of the car. That really surprised Jim, I think, like he never thought I had any of my own opinions or guts to tell him off. I guess the biggest thing that bugs me is that Mom and Dad suspect Nothing. They continue to think he's the perfect son, football star, and youth group leader all rolled up in one, when I can see right through him. I see him look nervously around in the back of the school where he parks so that he can light up before class. Sometimes I feel like his conscience.

We don't talk much when we ride to school these days. I used to try and make conversation, but Jim usually ignores me by pretending he doesn't hear me or by turning up the radio. Why bother? I'd rather be amused with my own thoughts, thank you. We pull up to this huge house with white pillars and a couple real nice cars parked in the driveway. Sitting Indian-style on a circle of grass in front of a statue of a naked boy with a jug on his shoulder is Jim's friend Keeler. He has on sunglasses and a black motorcycle jacket covered with chains. He looks up from a book he's reading, waves, and gets up slowly. I wonder why he's outside reading when there's still frost on the ground and it's about forty degrees.

He shuffles over to the car. Jim rolls down the window with the broken handle. It takes forever. I feel stupid in our Chevy Impala. The muffler is chugging.

"Nice car, pal," Keeler says, slapping the hood and walking around to get in.

"Whose BMW?" Jim asks.

"Mine. It's an old one I'm working on."

"Do you take it to school?"

"Yeah, usually. I just wanted to do the car pool thing for a change."

Jim laughs. "Seriously?"

"Well, I was sorta grounded from driving it for a week. You know how it goes. I appreciate the ride, though, man."

I sit in the front seat like the invisible woman. Keeler smells really great. It's patchouli oil, I think. All the hippy girls in my art class wear it. It's the only thing I can smell now in the car.

"Who's the girl up front there, Jim?"

Nice manners, Jim. Don't even introduce me!

"Oh, that's my sister, Sonny."

"Sonny? Sonny Bono?"

"It's Sonia," I say.

Keeler moves to the edge of his seat so that he's right behind my neck.

"Hmmmm. Sonja Henie? or Sonia Braga, the movie star?"

I don't know what to say. He's being obnoxious.

"Don't you have art fifth period?" he says.

I'm so embarrassed. When has he seen me in art? I'm sure, he asks all these questions. I feel stupid because I've never seen him in art before.

"Uh, I have art fourth period, but sometimes I stay during lunch," I gulp.

"Oh," he mumbles.

I want to keep talking to him to find out if he was in my class or if he knows any of the people in fourth period, but we're already in the parking lot when Keeler and Jim jump out of the car so fast and never say goodbye. Jim shuts off the engine, grabs his books, and pulls out a pack of cigarettes.

I stay in the car and check myself in the mirror. I want to see how I looked when Keeler was talking to me. I watch my brother and Keeler through the window. They stand there smoking away. Somehow, Keeler looks better with a cigarette between his lips than Jim. Jim looks like he's still learning or something. I hope they don't see me studying their smoking gestures. Keeler intrigues me. He sort of leans back against the car and exhales, like he's letting out all the stuff he thinks about. He isn't nervous like Jim. He looks like he could stand there all day smoking and saying nothing. Just watching the world go by.

I want to see him again. I want to see him in the hall and have him see me. I wonder if he would recognize me and say my name again the same way it sounded when he mumbled it behind my neck.

Jim

What's so square about carrying your Bible to church, son?" my dad said as we climbed aboard the family wagon.

"What?"

"I was just asking why you're not carrying your Bible with you this morning," my dad repeated. I'd heard him the first time.

"No big deal. I just didn't bring it along this morning—they have Bibles in the pews . . ."

My mother sighs and tries to give my dad a look. Then there's that car punishment silence that I hate. I wasn't in the mood for any debates on Bible-carrying speeches. The day had barely begun, and already I was getting condemned for something pretty small and picky. Hey, carrying a big leather Bible to church doesn't always make you feel any more of a huge Christian. According to Holly, last night I'm this sexual maniac who can't get enough.

Don't ask me what the sermon was about this morning. During the whole service I just sat there drifting back to Holly's driveway, feeling more and more anger at myself or toward her for being such a tease. Like I'm really the guilty one for pushing her too far. She can call it off and say, "*Stop!*" like she didn't *expect* one thing to lead to another. Hey, she was giving me the big signs last night. She knows she's hot. She knows exactly how to get what she wants and then "*Bam!*" she panics because she doesn't trust me. What did she think I was going to do? She gets out of the car like this piece of damaged waste, but I'm the one who's wanting something more. I try to feel sorry for not respecting her or whatever, but even though I feel bad, I can't really say I regret anything. In fact, when I start to think about Holly I don't know where to stop . . .

Whoa! I'm sitting next to my mom, and I'm thinking about sex. Then I start looking at the people up there in the choir, all the neatly groomed men all serious in the back rows and the sweet ladies staring into the audience—I think, "They've done it, probably." Those people up there have had sex! So why do I have to feel dirty about it?

Now I *do* feel guilty. I feel guilty because lately I might be lusting more after Holly instead of really thinking of her as my friend, as a girl with feelings and probably the same confused thoughts that I have. I'm just glad I don't have to see her today. I can't possibly call her. I wouldn't know what to say to her.

"Hello, Holly? Yeah, babe, I'm really digging you."

I'm just lucky I have to meet Keeler today. I can get out of the house so that I don't have to answer the phone. She'll call. Either that or she'll come over. She'll act all sweet to my parents, who love her and think she's this perfect Christian girl. If there was ever a problem, they'd never know it. Holly is a good faker. She'd never admit that, though.

Sometimes I wonder if my parents plan family devotions just to bug me. Is it necessary to read an entire chapter of the New Testament that takes a couple hours to read? I especially love it when you have somewhere to go in half an hour and you would really like to just eat and run but can't because you have to sit around the table after lunch and *participate* in these little family discussions and devotions. I never seemed to mind them when I was little. In fact all the stories and things we should learn to obey were easy to accept. I ate them up. And I was proud when I could spout a Bible verse. There was no time limit to my listening. I hadn't come up with other things that were more important yet. There were virtually no distractions. It's almost like I've outgrown the things I was taught, as if they were a suit or a pair of shoes. Sort of like they don't quite fit into my scene at high school all the time.

Dad initiates these talks by asking things like, "Sonia, how do you think this passage applies to your own life?"

So here we are sitting around the table after

lunch on Sunday afternoon, as though church isn't enough religion for one day. I look at the clock and it's two-fifteen, and devotions will take at least till two-forty-five because it's Sunday. I guess Sunday devotions are always longer to make up for rushing through them during the week.

"Dad, I was supposed to meet with this guy from my humanities class at two. Think we could make devotions short today?"

"Are you meeting Keeler?" Sonia asks.

"Yeah, we're on the same team for a debate we're having."

"You'll have plenty of time to meet your friend. Would you read for us please, Jim?" says Dad, handing me the Bible.

"Yeah, chapter five?"

I read to get through it. "So I say, live by the Spirit, and you will not gratify the desires of the sinful nature. For the sinful nature desires what is contrary to the Spirit, and the Spirit what is contrary to the sinful nature. They are in conflict with each other, so that you do not do what you want." The words leap out at me. My voice sounds strange, like I'm not the one who should be reading this. Then I have to get through this long list of sins. I check them off subconsciously.

"The acts of the sinful nature are obvious: sexual immorality, impurity and debauchery; idolatry and witchcraft; hatred, discord, jealousy, fits of rage, selfish ambition, dissensions, factions and envy; drunkenness, orgies, and the like."

Whew! Then I read the heavy part: "I warn

you, as I did before, that those who live like this will not inherit the kingdom of God."

I felt a discussion coming on. Dad hummed to himself. He was about to ask me what I thought of the passage I just read when I heard a car horn and some music booming in our driveway.

"Hey, maybe that's Keeler," I said, glad for the rescue.

"Jim, can you ask him to wait? We're not quite finished here yet," Mom said.

"C'mon, give me a break. What am I supposed to do? Just tell him to wait in the car while we have our family devotions for another forty-five minutes?"

I looked at Sonia for some help, but she was looking out the window. I wished she would speak up and argue, side with me once in a while. I'm always the antagonist. Doesn't she ever get tired of these contrived chats about our spiritual lives?

"Do you think we have devotions just to aggravate you, Jim? Your mother and I just want to know what's going on with you kids. We enjoy hearing what you think about, where you're at with the Lord."

"Well, can I be excused now so I don't keep Keeler waiting?"

"Why don't you invite him in for some cake?" my mom asks cheerfully. I hoped she was just trying to make a cute joke. I'm sure he'd really *enjoy* eating cake with my parents and sitting through a prayer that's a year long. Luckily my dad gave in and let me leave the table.

"Hey, man, was' up?" Keeler had his head leaning back against the headrest. He had his sunglasses on.

"Sorry you had to wait. I thought we were gonna meet at the restaurant," I said.

"I was bored, so I thought I would stop by and see if you wanted to study early. I thought you might be watching one of the football games on TV."

"Naah, we just finished eating," I said. I wasn't about to tell him we were doing devotions when he drove up. Now that I was with Keeler I really didn't know what to say. I didn't know him, I mean, I didn't know any people like him. Jocks don't usually mix with guys like Keeler, burnouts, or whatever.

"So you just moved here, right?"

"Yeah, Mom and Dad packed up the camper and here I am," Keeler smirked. "It's kind of a drag when you've lived somewhere all your life, and then one day you're supposed to say so long to all the friends you've ever had. This town's all right, I guess. I've never had to go to a private school before."

"Your parents *made* you go to Valley High?"

"Yeah, so I wouldn't get in trouble or something."

"Don't you like it?" I asked.

"Not really. It's pretty boring. Everyone seems so uptight about stuff."

"Yeah, I know." I wanted to tell him I was just as sick of Valley as he was. He probably thought I was this nice clean guy all involved in student council. Well, he's right. I pretty much live by the rules. He didn't say anything the rest of the way there, but I think I may've slipped and said something about school spirit once. He lighted up a cigarette and put in some tape, something really hardcore I'd never heard. It wasn't metal; it was probably some punk band.

I felt kind of nervous sitting in the restaurant with Keeler. Red Rooster is like this family restaurant diner place. Lots of families go there, families from my church who know me. I wanted to smoke really badly sitting there with Keeler, who was puffing away. We were in a big booth in the back and I didn't see any of the church crowd there, so I figured I'd be OK. I'd just have to be cool about watching the door. I wondered if Keeler went to church anywhere.

"So have you looked at any of this stuff?" Keeler asked with a mouth full of hamburger.

"Not really. Do you get it?" Keeler was wolfing down his food like he hadn't eaten in years. He was really involved in his food, like munching and nervously shoving it in. I felt like a big moron for not reading anything until today, but I really hadn't had time. I pulled out a cigarette.

"Great. This will be a real trip," Keeler said. "Hey, couldn't you get kicked off the team for smoking?"

"Yeah, but I haven't been caught so far," I said smoothly.

Keeler started into his explanation on determinism. It's like he totally changed gears and became this authoritative voice.

"Deterministic society is where there's already

an absolute set of facts that say things are going to be one set way. It's like fate, like you're going to choose what you choose because that was the way it was planned. People determine your fate for you, if you ask me," he said, "like your reputation is already implied because of your actions. Determinism can be like you will automatically decide to behave a certain way because your character or who you are is made by all the experiences you've had."

We sat there like a couple of huge scholars or something. I never thought about stuff like this. The stuff was blowing my mind.

"Yeah, but we can change our behavior or like choose not to do things that are harmful or bad. There are good choices that will help me be a better person and help other people, and then there are bad choices that bring everyone down, you know?" I said.

"Very good, O wise one, but who says there is one way as opposed to another way of doing something or of being? I know there's sinful behavior and then there's godly behavior, but if you say there is one necessary reality of what will be, like you will attain your ends by whatever means it takes, if there are only these parts that make up the whole big plan, then that rules out all the possibilities. You could just pessimistically give up and say, 'Oh well, it will happen this way anyway, so what say do I have?' It helps you not to regret stuff," he said. "Just go with the flow."

He had turned all mystified and was waving his french fries and cigarette for emphasis. I had never pictured Keeler caring much about serious stuff like philosophy. He acted like he loved this, like he was trying to prove something.

"That isn't only it . . . it's not just our actions being preordered," I said. "I want to know what makes someone choose. Your motive has to come from somewhere. Maybe your desires or who you are, are determined."

"So then we can't help who we are?" Keeler asked. "I don't believe that. We're free to improve who we are. You're right, we have our personality and everything, but maybe our experiences make us who we turn out to be. Hey, man, look at me."

I leaned forward. "So what about like a murderer? What does he say, 'Oh, I'm sorry I shot a man—I couldn't help it, that's the way I am.' " I laughed at my humorous joke. I wanted to lighten things up, take a break, maybe.

"It seems like the only reason you don't do stuff is because if you do, you'll be punished for it. You don't want to get in trouble. That could be a motive," he said, trailing off.

"This stuff is pretty heavy," I said, tapping my cigarette on an ashtray. "It seems pretty obvious that man is free and not a robot. I mean, God gave us the ability to choose."

Keeler blew some smoke. "See, most people at our school think there's a certain code of behavior—a way of dressing and acting so that no one steps out and acts different. I don't get it. Who says? Who's the one that sets the restrictions? That's what stepping out of the plan is—like our school. If you do your own thing, have a little bit of a crazy idea about something, you get accused of being a rebel or a bat from hell. Seriously, man, people need to live like they want."

Just then I saw Mr. and Mrs. Camfeld and their son walk in, a reminder back in reality. There was no way they could've seen me, but I snuffed my cigarette in the ashtray anyway. Mrs. Camfeld was friends with my mom, they did these women's things, and she had a big mouth. I mean, I'm sure if she saw me smoking she would think I had completely rejected every value, every sermon, everything that I was supposed to be. I was sick of talking about all this choice and free-will garbage. I didn't feel like slamming on my school, yet I knew what Keeler meant about uptight people. I used to be uptight. More uptight than I am now, actually. I don't know if that's good or bad. I mean being more aware of your conscience. I remember the first time I heard one of the guys on the team swear. I was shocked and felt like I should talk to him about his language. That makes me want to laugh now about what a geek I was.

Keeler tried to get the waitress's attention. He leaned out of the booth and batted at her as she passed by. He wanted coffee.

"Hey, why don't you just leave the pot here?" She gave him a strange look, and he smiled sweetly. "I love coffee."

"Let's take a break, man, whaddaya say? That's a pretty sound argument." Keeler slammed his books shut and packed up. "I think I'll wear my zoot suit to this presentation thing. That would be a hoot."

"Yeah, that will throw those determinists off. I get it. That just proves there's no set dress code," I said.

Keeler was lighting one match after another. He had gone through all the matches in the pack. As I sat there watching each flame go down, almost to his fingertips, I was thinking about getting burned and becoming truly symbolic. I was thinking some cliché my dad would say: You play with fire and you'll get burned.

Sonia

I wanted to see Keeler in the hall to get a good long look at him. I guess I really didn't get a chance to study him when I met him in the car. A quick look over my shoulder and then through the car window while he was smoking. Jim hasn't picked him up for school since then even though I've tried to ask Jim about him. Jim doesn't give me much information. I just want to know what he's like. I was even nervous today when I went to art fourth period. I half-expected to see him in my class, but he wasn't there.

I thought I would stay up in the loft during lunch to finish my self-portrait, which I hate. I like the life-drawing section we're doing in class now. I just don't enjoy drawing *my* life. Me. The sketch I'm working on is embarrassing. I don't know how I could possibly make myself look any worse, except in real life!

I'm sitting here munching on my tuna sandwich and carrots and staring at this pencil drawing of myself. I don't feel like working on it. I have a mirror here so I can study my features. Maybe the mirror isn't working. I feel so jumpy, listening for someone on the stairs, like any minute Keeler could come in and find me here and see me by myself with my portrait. Today is the first time I've felt stupid about being antisocial at lunch. If Keeler came up here he might ask me why I wasn't eating lunch with my friends, and then I might accidentally tell him that I couldn't really decide where I fit in or what group of people to hang out with. I might tell him that I liked to work alone with my tapes playing, shutting everything out. He'd think I was some kind of loner or plague. That would be really bad.

Holly gave me her opinion of Keeler. She came over yesterday. I know she stopped over to see her little "pooh bear," my brother, who wasn't home. I think he actually blew her off so he could study with Keeler. She acted like that's what happened anyway. She was really upset. She acted nice and polite in front of my mom, eating her cake and full of grown-up conversation, but after we finished dessert, when I had shut the door to my room, she exploded.

"I can't believe Jim! Thanks, Jim. Just blow me off. He told me last night he would help me plan the Halloween party I'm having."

She stood in front of my mirror pouting and doing this whole speech to herself. She like performed it dramatically with these hysterical facial expressions. It didn't seem like she was talking to me at all. She was rehearsing.

"Where did Jim go, do you know?" She whipped around to face me, letting her blond hair fly.

"He's studying for his humanities debate with this guy Keeler," I said evenly.

"Oh, great! They're on the same team. I thought Jim and I would work together, but Jim didn't say anything and I ended up with this guy who doesn't have a clue about life. I think Jim wanted to work with Keeler or something. Do you know Keeler?"

"Uh, not really. Jim gave him a ride the other day. He seemed pretty cool," I said. I really wanted to tell her that I thought he was gorgeous and that I'd go out with him in a second.

"He's a big druggie. I'm surprised Jim went with him. Jim will sure work well with a guy whose brain is fried half the time," she said, rolling her eyes.

"You don't even know this guy. How do you know what he does? I thought he was OK when I met him," I said. "You're just worried about what people will say, aren't you?"

Holly gave me a look of utter disgust. I suddenly felt very stupid. Why should Holly care what I thought of Keeler when she barely talked to me at school or at Senior High Club? The truth was that she only associated with me when it involved Jim: football games, Pep Squad, parties. If Jim was with her she'd include me, but I could never just walk up to her group of friends and feel like I was welcome. Yet

I continued to be in awe of her because I wanted so badly to know how I could be like her.

"Did you and Jim have fun last night?" I asked. I was such a swell sister. Like she'd really fill me in on all the details!

"Why, did Jim say something to you?" Holly asked.

"No, he didn't tell me anything. Why, did something happen?"

"No . . ." She paused like she wanted to tell me whatever it was that happened; then she totally changed the subject. "Do these jeans make me look huge?"

"You look great in them. Quit flattering yourself," I said. I was always telling her how good she looked.

"So do you want to help me with my party? I already found an old prom formal of my mom's from the fifties that I'm going to wear," Holly said, moving in on my closet. She held up my clothes against her, then tossed them back on their rack. There was nothing in my closet she would want, yet every time she was over she did this, like she was discarding me.

I ended up saying Yes to her party planning. It's so weird. I know she didn't come over to talk to me. Jim wasn't home, so she asked me. I never know when someone is using me, like Holly. I should just quit being paranoid and relax.

Lunch is over now. I guess I haven't really done much on my drawing and I haven't seen Keeler, who is the real reason I stayed up here today. It'll happen, though. We'll meet up here one day and that will be it. We'll realize that we're totally perfect for each other and maybe, if I'm feeling extremely brave, I can invite Keeler to Holly's party. Yeah, and I'm sure Holly would just love that!

Holly

I've been staring out the window at the flaming orange-and-red trees for the past fifteen minutes. I try to study in first period study hall, I really do, but it's always so hot in the room and I'm not really a morning person, particularly this morning; I'm nervous about seeing Jim in humanities. He hasn't called me since the hayride, and since Sunday, when he blew me off to go with Keeler, I've been convinced that he's bored with me or thinks I'm some pristine virgin who can't have any fun. I looked for him when I got to school this morning. We're always together by his locker before first period. He's avoiding me, I know it.

All around me are the unconscious victims of study hall. Everyone in here has their head on their desks or on their folded arms on top of their books. I'm lucky Sandra and Debbie sit near me, or I would die in this wasteland, staring out the window at the trees changing color and at the horrible church cemetery that faces the school. Talk about depressing! Try getting through calculus looking at the exact same view on a day when the sky isn't even gray, but sort of a dirty white.

A folded note hits the floor by my desk. I reach down and slowly scoop it up. Debbie has her head bowed over her homework but is watching me with a sly smile. Mrs. Moorehouse, the study hall monitor, isn't watching us at the moment. She usually picks on us especially because we're cheerleaders. She says we "need to save our rah-rah-rah for the games." She coaches the girls' athletic teams, so that's probably why. Her girls are the athletes and the good students. We're just the popular airheads.

I unfold the note from Debbie.

"Are your Parents going to be home when you have the party? Do you think there's a way you could get them to be out that night? We could have it just couples (you and Jim, me and Dave, Sandra and Jeff) Is it for your youth group? Do you have to invite the freshman and those gross girls that were at the ice cream thing that one night? We could make it more romantic with just couples and guys from the team. Forget about games and songs and stuff, I say we light some candles and Play Around! -D"

I stared at the note. It was exactly what Mom and I had fought about this morning. I didn't know what to do. Mom got all suspicious when I asked her if I could give the party. I didn't know exactly how to ask her without turning it into something obviously conniving. So I asked her nicely, "Don't you think I'm old enough to have a party where my parents aren't . . . I mean, you're not youth sponsors, and Coach will probably stop by anyway."

Right away my mom says, "Will you be doing things that you don't want us to find out about?" My mom makes me so mad. She actually *makes* me want to do something really reckless so that she'll appreciate what a wonderful daughter she has—one who hasn't ever given her any cause to worry. I just gave up and left for school. She assured me that she and Dad will be sure and stay out of sight so that I won't be ashamed or embarrassed.

Great. So how can I make my party look like it will be the kind that Debbie and Sandra would approve of? I feel the pressure, but I know I will never be like the total party queen. Drinking and sleeping around the school are things I don't have to have to be cool. I'll never be into it. I just wish I could say that instead of trying to pretend that scene doesn't bother me.

I'm not even sure Jim and I will still be together by that time. I decided not to tell Debbie yet about my parents being home. There was nothing I could do to make my parents any different. They would never be as laid-back as Debbie's. She had parties all the time, and her parents were always out of town. I would just let her think it was "that kind of party," and she'd have to deal with it later when she'd find out it wasn't.

I sent the note back up the row.

"D- That sounds great! I had the exact same idea. Be good—'The House' is watching! -H."

Apparently "The House" *had* been watching us because after the bell rang I started to pass her desk, which sat like a watchtower up on this platform thing when she stopped me.

"Ummm, Ms. Dade? I know you don't think I see you and your girlfriends passing the notes back and forth, but I do. So unless you really enjoy this classroom, I would suggest that you stick to your work, or you'll be spending more time in here after school."

"Yes, ma'am," I said. She was the ugliest woman I knew of, and I tried very hard not to show her my hate.

"Oh, and could you pass that message on to your friends?" she added.

"Sure will," I said cheerfully, slipping out the door.

Now I *really* wasn't ready to deal with Jim and Keeler in humanities. I wasn't ready for any of Jim's attitudes or little games. He had probably already told Keeler about me.

The bell had already rung as I sat there in my little group with my partner John. I was waiting for Jim and Keeler, who weren't there yet, the losers.

Mr. Cardigan was answering questions about the assignment when the boys shuffled in. They sat down, trying to look sincere while holding back their laughter. They reeked of smoke. I didn't look at Jim. I was afraid I'd

43

glare a hole through his body.

"We've got the conference room at ten-thirty so we can start practicing," said Becky, who had done nothing for the project so far.

Jim and Keeler hunched over their desks and looked completely blank.

"I don't think we're ready for that. How are you guys coming?" I asked. I hoped they weren't prepared because I sure wasn't ready to defend myself. Was it my imagination, or was Keeler staring at my chest?

"We just got started," Keeler mumbled.

No one was talking in our group. All the other groups' voices rose and fell into a drone. Why did I have to lead this group anyway? "Maybe we could work better in the library," I suggested.

So we all got up, glad for the change of scenery, and paraded to the library. Walking out the door, Keeler asked me if I was using the King James.

"Bible?" I stuttered and then I realized he meant, Am I using a Bible for the debate. "Yeah, I guess." Keeler was trying to make me look stupid. I saw him give Jim a knowing look. I remembered how Jim used to focus his attention on me. It was like it was just us that mattered. No one else could interrupt. We had this space that was ours, and if anyone came too near they would know that it was time to leave. That wasn't what was happening now. I was the one left out.

Jim walked along with me down the hall. I waited for him to say something. I wanted to talk to him without Keeler nearby.

"I hear you stopped by yesterday," he said.

"We were supposed to get together, remember?"

"I'm sorry. It's just that Keeler and I wanted to get started on the project."

"Is that also why you were late for class?" I heard myself sound like my mother, like a nagging wife.

Keeler answered for Jim, like I was really talking to him. "That's my fault," he said.

And I thought, "Wait. You don't have to answer for Jim. He has a brain and he's responsible to make his own decisions, and besides, he's not going to get away with blaming you for blowing me off."

"This is more than a project for you, isn't it, Keeler?" I blurted.

"Sure it is. This is free will and determinism here. This is a big game for me," he said in a snappy voice.

"Um, Jim we need to talk. I mean, not about free will and determinism, we need to talk about stuff. You know . . ." I said, ignoring Keeler.

"OK, OK, we will. Later. It's cool. We'll talk."

He has managed to shut me up, or Keeler has, and the practice goes terribly even with the change of scenery.

CHAPTER

8

Sonia

No amount of studying could possibly help me pass an algebra test. I'm serious. I am convinced that I have some sort of mental blockage in the area of math. My brain registers a blank screen full of white fuzzy static. A flashing red light appears that reads, "Needs Help! Seek Tutor."

I had gone past the anxiety stages for my exam during last period in history, where I futilely reviewed by paging through the different chapters and staring at the polynomials and integers, hoping they would leap into my head and work themselves out without me. Entering the exam I was paralyzed and trancelike. I looked at the girls around me who were going over sample problems they had carefully worked out. Like these girls needed to worry or review at all! I was feeling hostile and foolish. They should know I sat for two hours at the kitchen

46

table with my mother, the only person patient enough to do math with me in subremedial language: SUBTRACT = TO TAKE AWAY.

The last exam I had tried to cheat on. I had a tiny formula sheet on the floor sticking out of my notebook. But the little "helps" were no helps at all, and I ended up with a D. I can't even cheat well!

When Mr. Felzler handed me my test I could almost see a faint look of doubt or mocking in his already droopy eyes. This was the kind of test where you could begin with Part I or IV and not have it matter. I chose to work the test backward since every question looked completely foreign. I looked around the classroom. Everyone was working out the problems in long steps on scratch paper. I stared at all the empty space where we were to "show our work." I invented some set-ups using at least the numbers that were given. I chewed my gum furiously and began on my nails. I stared at Mr. Felzler sitting like Father Time grading his papers. I tried to send him signals for sympathy. More time passed and my eyes wandered further.

I started to zoom in on the test of a girl sitting diagonally from me. I tried to examine her work to get some answers. I hoped I was reading them clearly and began copying them. At least I was doing something to fill in the time besides squirming pitifully in my desk seat and raking my hair. There were forty-five minutes still left. I had gone through the test pages over and over randomly filling in the space under the problems, like I could add just one more number under a problem just for flare!

I decided I was finished. I had left a few blank questions, but I didn't care to stay any longer. Obviously there wasn't going to be any miraculous intervention. Besides, maybe the class would think I had finished early because the test was so easy and I had gotten an A. Probably not, though. Anyone who saunters up front that early has obviously given up and failed.

I wandered out of school before the last bell of the day. I felt oddly conspicuous, like I was fleeing from something no one else knew about. It was a relief to be out in the late afternoon light and air of chilly October, though it was a false relief, knowing I didn't deserve to be out of the harsh fluorescent light, unlocking my bike before my classmates had finished their tests. But I was leaving and wouldn't be convinced to return to my test with all its mistakes and equations without answers.

As I rode away from school it never occurred to me where I was really riding until I was weaving along streets in Englewood, which happens to be the neighborhood where Keeler lives. I wasn't planning on meeting him. I hadn't even taken my bike home that way before. I just ended up there, passing houses and yards that meant nothing to me except that they were part of Keeler's everyday route. I thought I was lost. That was all I needed—to be accidently lost in Keeler's neighborhood and have him come driving home from school to pass me, the happy wanderer, craning my neck for a look at his house. I recognized the houses now. They were getting bigger. I didn't want to stop in front of his house. I was afraid I might get off my bike and sit on his lawn. Then I might start crying, sitting there out of place until Keeler would come home, find me, and welcome me because I looked so lost and sad all by myself.

So I stopped my bike. I figured as long as I had taken the Keeler tour trip home I might as well take a long look at his house. There were no signs of Keeler except for a beat-up car that was parked under a big oak tree in the front yard. The car looked ridiculously out of place in front of the majestic house on the neatly land-scaped property. I spotted the stone statue of the naked boy with the jug. It made me think of Keeler, though I couldn't think why except that it made me laugh. Keeler had probably placed the statue there for a joke thinking it would shock people.

I didn't think I should wait around anymore. I turned my bike back and left. Riding through the neighborhood was a performance now, I suppose, because Keeler could be watching me.

A few days later I was up in the art loft again. I wasn't waiting for Keeler to visit. I didn't want to keep planning meetings since I had been disappointed every day I had tried to spot him. I don't think things happen when you try to plan them out, but then maybe if I was more bold I could get some guys' attention and make them notice me.

I was thinking about guys while I was work-ing on my portrait again. I wondered how peo-ple really saw me. Like what do I look like to other people? Am I better or worse than what I think? Our new assignment was to take the picture we had already done of ourselves and distort it in some way. I thought that was pretty dumb since I already had a distorted-looking portrait to work with anyway. It wasn't a very image-boosting assignment, but I kind of enjoyed crossing my eyes and giving myself a bigger mouth.

"You are my sunshine, my only sunshine," someone sang from the bottom of the stairs. It scared me at first. I had been in my own little world and forgotten I was alone. The voice laughed and said my name again in this faraway ghost voice. It was Keeler and he was starting up the stairs. I suddenly didn't know how to act. I had pictured this so many times, how I wanted it to happen, that I forgot what I had me saying in the dream. I almost said, "Where have you been? I've been looking all over for you."

"Sonia, you're skipping lunch," Keeler said. He was standing right behind me looking over my shoulder. I stared at my picture in front of me. I'm sure he was looking at it too.

"Yeah, I'm getting behind in life drawing class. It's my favorite class, but I'm never happy with my eyes."

"You have terrific eyes," Keeler said. I turned around a little, but I couldn't really look at him. Now that he was actually standing there and we were all alone I wondered what he had in mind.

"Gee, thanks," I kidded. "So what are you up to?"

"Oh, I'm just wandering the halls, looking for trouble, bored out of my skull," he said, rolling his eyes. I got a quick look at him. He looked really pale. His hair was all tussled and kind of hung over his eyes. He had a habit of flicking his head back, whipping the hair away. He was wearing the black jacket I had seen before. It was like a second skin on him.

"This would be a great place for a rock video, dude," he said, looking around the loft. He started strutting around like he was a per-former, drumming on the desks and walls. I just watched him and laughed. "Am I hot or what? Huh? Huh?" he shouted. I wasn't sure what he was going to do next. The bell rang and I gathered up my stuff. Keeler was sitting on the banister watching me and grinning.

"You look like this girl I knew," he said sol-emnly. "She had this cattish face and I always used to meow at her. That's not an insult. That's good. She was a swell gal."

Keeler seemed to say anything he felt like saying. Like he wasn't afraid to come out and say that I looked like a cat or whatever. I guess that was supposed to mean he liked me. I thought that until he started joking with me that I was Jim's little sister. I couldn't get away from that title, not even with someone as cool as Keeler.

"How do you know Jim?" I asked as we went down the stairs.

"We're in humanities together. He's the token jock of the intellectual freedom committee."

"What?"

"His girlfriend thinks her desk is a pulpit," he said, waiting for a response. I couldn't tell if Keeler was serious or not. He was leaning on one of the tables and drumming out a beat.

"You mean Holly? Keeler, that's not very fair since you don't even know her."

He didn't say anything. Maybe he thought I was a Holly type and had lost interest. I wondered if there was a chance of getting together with Keeler again.

"Maybe you could get to know Holly better by coming to her Halloween party." I looked around the room and at the floor. Keeler had already gotten off the table and was headed for the door. I couldn't believe I had just invited him to Holly's party.

"I don't think so," he said, wrinkling up his nose. He gave me one last look and a little wink. "Take it easy, babe," he said, and was gone.

I just sat there unable to move. I almost followed him out, but I didn't want to seem like a puppy. I had this feeling we could maybe be friends. Something told me he was a dangerous one to get close to, but . . . I liked that. I liked surprises.

Jim

Busted, man," Steve said, throwing his towel at my face. "Coach said he wanted to see you in his office."

So there I was, sitting in Coach's little hole of an office, staring at towels, trophies, and every piece of sports equipment ever invented. There were team pictures, pictures of Coach in action, and all kinds of plaques, which made me nostalgic, like I was in the hall of fame or something. I was sure I was facing the end of my football career. Coach had finally found out I smoked. Either that or my grades were as bad as I feared. He was taking forever to see me. It was like waiting for the doctor. I thought I heard him whistling outside the door. That was a good sign at least.

"Hey, Jim," Coach said, dumping his clip-board and whistle and taking a seat in his leather recliner. He was doing the pep-talk positive-attitude tone of voice that reminded me of my dad saying, "Hey, pal," or "Hey, sport." So what do you say when you think you're about to get a speech?

He took a deep breath. "You look good out there, Jim. I've watched how you've played this season and you've really improved. Your spirit on the team has really pulled the guys together in tough times. Some of the other coaches have noticed that too," he paused. "Jim, I don't want to come down hard on you, but as your youth pastor at church I don't see quite the same spirit or attitude. I know you're a senior and some of the activities and group things might be getting a little old, but I sense that you've really dropped out of discussions. Well, you're just not as verbal about your Christian life as you used to be. Kids in our group really look up to you, Jim. You're the star football player, you're easygoing, smart, you've got a lot going for you. Believe it or not, you're watched. Kids will listen to what you have to say."

I sat there all serious. I would've much rather had Coach talk to me about football or even have warned me about smoking instead of a talk about being a shining example for my youth group. It suddenly hit me how I was just supposed to be this thing, this Nice Guy who could never do anything or say anything unexpected. Coach was just assuming that Jim Peterson would always be the boy standing in front of his church eager and excited about the great new impact he would make on his school since going to winter camp. Yeah, I was that person once. Like what I've said about growing out of a suit or a pair of shoes—it happens. Things aren't always going to fit you. So why couldn't I sit back and let someone else be the leader for a change? Do other guys have to sit through this speech, or am I the only one?

After Coach had finished his talk I prayed there wouldn't be more. He asked me if there were any personal problems I might want to share with him. Share. What on earth does *share* mean? I did *not* want to share. I wanted to leave without any questions. I politely told Coach that I would try and be more aware of others, that I probably just had a lot on my mind lately, thinking about college and all. That seemed to satisfy him.

"OK, Jim, we'll see you at practice then tomorrow. You're a great kid; I just don't want you to blow your stand for Christ by worrying about being cool."

It was times like these, when you weren't quite sure who you were, when someone had summed you up, that you might like a close friend to say, "Hey, forget about it. They don't understand you, but I do." And that person would usually have been Holly, but she wouldn't be that person today. She would be on Coach's side, agreeing that I was trying hard to be someone else, shutting people out.

The other day after Holly's huff in class she scheduled this talk. We went to Red Rooster for one stiff hour of disagreeing, and then I drove her home. She basically told me that Keeler was a bad influence. I told her people don't understand Keeler. And they don't. She's a perfect example. Right away she says he uses drugs. That's all she knows about him. Keeler hasn't even mentioned drugs. I said she should be more tolerant. "Tolerance doesn't mean carelessness, Jim. What is it you're keeping your mind open to?"

I told her my mind was open to life. Is that so bad? If she would just go back to letting me live like I live without commentary, I would love to see her right now. She can be such a sweet girl.

I was sitting on the cold cement steps outside school, the most popular place to sit during breaks. These steps are always full. It's the place to watch others, to slice them down, look them over, and make some kind of a comment. This is the place to make yourself seen in your scene with the people you call your friends. Of course I would need a smoke after a speech on my reputation. I wasn't exactly anxious to get home. I was still a bit nervous after the talk from Coach, and I wasn't ready for any more examination from Mom or Dad.

I heard the sound of girls' twittering voices from the side of the building. Before I had a chance to rub out my cigarette, Holly spotted me and came skipping up. I let my arm dangle and flicked it in the grass. Holly looked good. She glowed from cheerleading practice and actually seemed glad to see me. I tried not to look horrified.

"How was practice?" she said, delivering a nice kiss on my cheek.

"Easy. Coach was in a good mood today," I lied.

"Have you been smoking?" She noticed the smoke and drew away like I was a leper. I don't know how I had kept the big secret for this long, but I guess I had been careful. Right now it didn't seem to matter. If she was going to find things about me to criticize, this was another one. Smoking just came with the whole lousy package.

"Keeler smokes," I fumbled. "No biggie." I was really groping now. What a low way to cover— blame it on my new friend.

"Not you?"

"Well, if I feel like it," which being interpreted meant only a pack a day whenever I can break away for a cancer stick.

"Jim, you could get kicked off the team for that!"

"I don't do it that much. Wait. Who made you my mother? Why do you suddenly annoy me? And what's the big deal with you and Keeler? Are you jealous?"

"Oh, come on, Jim. Boy, are you a little sensitive." Holly looked like I had hit her.

I felt no pity for her and her puppy dog eyes. I wasn't finished telling her off. "Did it ever occur to you that I might have friends who are different from you? Do you ever associate with anyone who's not even remotely a part of your world?" There. I had said it. I couldn't believe how insane I was.

"That's enough, Jim. Are you through? I hope you feel better now," she said, walking away. It was the first time I hadn't given her a ride home.

CHAPTER

10

Keeler

Not too many people know I live in my car. I'm serious. This is where I sleep. My dad and his wife Judy gave me these lovely options: Either I decide I'm going to join the family for dinner and stop staying out all night, or I will stay out of the house. Courtesy is what it's all about, they say. Another thing they bring up that has to do with the main reason I sleep in the car is that they know about my "dope habit." First of all, if you're going to tell me what I do, don't call it dope. That's not the word.

One day about a month ago I came home from school really buzzed. I had smoked with a few guys in the park after school, and it must've been some nasty stuff. I was starved when I got home. I just wanted to eat and be left to my own demented existence. I came into the kitchen and there was Judy, my stepmom, sitting at the table with her soap operas on, reading beauty magazines.

"Hey, Judy. Don't you ever do any housework?" I groaned.

I could tell that totally shocked her because she tightened her mouth up and her face got all tight too. Her hair was fanning out in all directions. She was trying to look chic or something by styling her hair way out. I suddenly got hit with this hysterical picture of a dog. She looked like a dog, a puzzled dog. It was so intense I started laughing and repeating, "Pomeranian." I was howling with laughter until I felt sick.

"What are you on?" she panicked. "I am going to call your father in from the garden, Keeler. Now stop it." She scolded me like I was a bad boy. I honestly didn't care. She didn't know why I was laughing.

Judy brought my father in. By that time I had chilled way down and was sitting there watching two people in bed on the TV with the sound turned down. I was exhausted.

"Judy tells me you came home high on something. Is that true?" my father asked in his "no two ways about it" voice.

"Dad, I'm in a good mood; is that OK? Can I laugh?"

"You have insulted Judy and I have reason to believe that you are taking drugs or something. You're not yourself, Keeler. What's going on with you?"

"Nothing. I'm just having fun," I mumbled.

So later they gave me this ultimatum. They

couldn't prove I smoked pot, but my behavior showed it, and they were tired of hearing me come home at weird hours. They were sure I was in with a bad crowd. I was to sleep in the car, but I could get ready and eat in the house before school. I don't know why I haven't just left home, since I can't live there.

I guess that would just be too depressing. Besides, this can't last long since it's getting colder now at night.

It's a Friday night, and here I am in my upholstered world with no major plans and I'm actually scared. I'm jumpy or something. This night is set up like a horror movie. The wind is blowing, the tree branches look like hands, and my windshield is getting covered with dead leaves. I'm staking out my own house. I can watch an entire evening of events pass in the lives of Jack and Judy. Jack is locked in for an evening of fine viewing in the family room. The entire room is dark except for the pale blue glow that wobbles from the television screen. He's most likely asleep, his head on his hand in his big chair. Rats, I wish I were there to see that.

Judy hates the dark, so I'm sure she's upstairs where the light's on in the bedroom. She's no doubt rented a video for herself and is already in bed waiting for Jack. If a prowler found me out here in my car, my shouting wouldn't even be heard above the sound of the TVs. I don't know why I don't just go out. Partying alone can be a drag. Drag, man, am I funny!

After last night I'm not sure how soon I'll trust myself to go out stoned again. I went over to Hyperspace, this video arcade. I always go there, no problem, I mean, the kids there are OK. They're not looking for trouble. You just mind your own business, which is what I do anyway because I get on a game, and it's like I can't stop for anything because I want to beat my scores and I can work out all my tension that way.

A few seconds after I got there I was worried. I took my stroll around the place a couple times, just looking things over, and I knew what games I wanted. I just wanted to look like I was looking for a challenge. I didn't want to just go to the same game automatically. But I felt like someone was watching me, really. I couldn't concentrate. I didn't want to look around because if I saw the person I would probably be in trouble right then. It's my face. People just don't like my face. When I finally did turn around to find the set of eyes, I didn't see anyone at first. But then I saw this shaggy-looking black guy sitting on a swivel chair by the snack bar with this girl in a fringe jacket. They were both looking at me. I quick went back to my game, which was running out. I'm not too good at confrontation, and I couldn't just leave, or they would've probably followed me out to the mall, so I went over to them.

I started out real smart-aleck, tough guy, "Look. I couldn't help noticing, but is there like something you want?"

The guy acted surprised. "Me, man? We're

just looking around."

The girl gave him a quick look. She was real sleazy looking with tons of eyeliner and lipstick.

"But, brother, I think there might be something you want," the guy said in a hypnotic voice. He called himself Jamaican Bob, I think. I might have called him the wrong names. I think I called him Kenyan Bob or Zulu Bob. Anyway, he had this great hash mix that he sold me. I don't know how he picked me out; it was kinda spooky. He told me later that Tracy, the girl, was the one who spotted me. She was on me right away like a maggot. I'm so upset that I don't remember what we did. She had a huge gap in her front teeth that I wanted to fill in. Every time I close my eyes I see her dark face and the laughing teeth between her sloppy burgundy lips. Man, I must've been really wasted. I know I went to this garage or hut. There were fringed pillows all over and not much else except a couple of foam beds that just looked like more pillows. Tracy made me listen to this demo tape of her singing. The whole experience was really painful. Her voice sounded like a small crying child with a tantrum, and the accompaniment was a lot of zither or sitar or whatever that Indian music is. It just made my head vibrate.

When I woke up I still had my clothes on, at least, but I realized I was late for school. Bob and Tracy were asleep on the pillows. I was sure my car was still at the mall, which was who knows where from the garage place. I felt like I could have some kind of disease. I had spent the night with people I didn't even know. If I had done anything to or with Tracy it wasn't the first time she'd had it, but who knows where she'd been? I tiptoed out of their hut, sure I wouldn't be seeing them again. I was very lucky their place was in an area I recognized. Too bad it was about five miles from the mall. I must've looked like a gross piece of trash walking at a shaky pace on the side of the road. It was rush hour and the traffic moved along as fast as I was walking. I'm sure I was an amusing sight for all the corporates glancing over at me.

Just thinking about myself that way makes me want to cry and laugh at the same time. Cry because I think I might be lonely and laugh because I live so dangerously and usually manage to luck out. Like when I reached the parking lot I laughed when I saw my little car hunched there like a roach. It was waiting for me right where I parked it when I left with two strangers about a million hours ago. Yet back to the lonely part. I guess I'd like to see what it's like to be straight for one day and let someone get to know me. One person comes to mind. Well, two, I guess. Jim and his sister Sonny. Well, Jim's just a nice guy, but his sister is such an angel. That sounds queer to say. What I mean is that it's comforting to know that there are kind, straight chicks like her. I'm not going to wake up in the middle of the night and shudder at the thought of her face, put it that way. Look, I've been with girls more in the camp of Tracy from last night. Thinking thoughts of Sonny makes me less afraid here in my car in the wind and the rain.

11

Holly

When I woke up this morning I thought there was a reason I should feel sad. I turned over in my tangle of sheets and tried hard to come up with the reason. Then I remembered. "I may have lost my best friend. I may have lost Jim."

The dream I woke out of was a real downer. It was so real I thought I heard myself crying in my sleep. It was the kind of dream where you blink your eyes to get out of it as if you can stop the cameras and the action. I was at my Halloween party running around making sure everyone was having a good time. The awful thing was that I was panicked because I didn't recognize anyone in their costumes. I couldn't tell if they were invited or not, and they weren't just in cutesy costumes, either; they were all pretty gruesome and surrounded me in my living room. I was going up to each person and asking them if they were Jim. "Has anyone seem Jim? Is anyone of you here Jim?" I circled the room, but no one would help me, and I stood there in the middle of the room with all the masks and makeup and cried.

Real life seemed just as unreal as my dream. When I got off the bus I headed straight for the girl's bathroom. That's where I know I can find Debbie and Sandra each morning. We all sort of get ready together and share each other's makeup and redo our hair and stuff. The bathroom was unusually crowded. There were all these scummy girls hanging out and a few smoking in the stalls. I couldn't talk to Sandra and Deb with all those girls clinging around. Usually it was just us and the tiles, our own dressing room.

"Hi, chick. How's your mood?" Sandra said. "Sorry I didn't call when I heard about you and Jim, but Jeff was over and we were busy."

"That's OK. I'm fine. It's just weird. Have you seen him yet?"

"No, we haven't seen the creep. He's probably with his new group of friends," Debbie said, leaning into the mirror. "But we have a better choice for you, right, San?"

Sandra had her head upside down and was letting all her hair fall as she brushed it briskly. Her hair was so gorgeous. She had this naturally curly hair that needed no curling. I was tempted to start on my beauty treatment, but I had already spent two hours getting ready at home for no reason. Debbie was trying a rainbow effect with her eyeshadows.

"What's your choice?" I asked. I knew it must be a guy.

"Chuck Zyder thinks you're hot," Sandra announced to the whole bathroom. "I told him you broke up with Jim. He's eager, Hol . . ."

"But we didn't break up. We just had a fight, and I'm not sure what that means. I know I don't feel like seeing Jim, but I don't know . . ." I babbled.

"So you're not interested in Chuck? Now's your chance. Listen, any jock who's mixing with a stoner like Keeler doesn't know what he wants. Forget him," Debbie said.

"Thanks a lot. Woo! Chuck Zyder. Z-man, huh?" I said.

"Yeah, invite him to your party quick while things are still bad with Jim," Sandra said, swinging her purse and books out the door in a cloud of perfume.

"I know a night with Z-man would cheer me up—then go back to Jim later if you still miss him," Debbie said.

I came out of the bathroom like I was making an entrance. I had this new feeling of freedom and possibility like I was still OK even without Jim by my side. If I'm really the determinist I claim to be in our debate project, maybe I should believe that Jim and I weren't meant to be! Just as I was thinking my new thoughts of freedom I looked up and saw I was walking straight toward Chuck and his friends, who were also all Jim's friends. Jim was usually with them, or I was usually with Jim. I suddenly felt naked or clumsy by myself. I wasn't what people expected to see. I was Holly without Jim. But there was Chuck and he was definitely looking at me. I smiled shyly, but that was all I would let myself do. I was more interested in knowing what Jim was doing this morning without me.

Another overcast day and I hadn't seen Jim. He must have some new place to hide or some new route to class. We didn't have humanities on Fridays, and that was my only class with him. This was the first Friday afternoon when I climbed the bus without any great plans for a wild weekend. I was baby-sitting, and you know your social life is over when you end up baby-sitting on a Friday night. It's not just for money, either; it's because you actually have no plans. No dates. I hoped this embarrassing fact wouldn't reach too many people.

When I got to the Piedmonts' house I was horrified to learn they had a baby. I had only remembered a little boy, but then that just shows how long it's been since I've had to baby-sit for these people. So now I have two brats to take care of.

I was afraid of babies. I didn't know how to hold them. My mom always told me to watch the head. So like when the baby's head is rolling all around, what could happen? Maybe it could just fall back and bounce onto the floor?

The mother gave me instructions that I thought she should've left in a manual by the phone or something.

"These are Melody's vitamins. She likes a bottle of milk before bedtime. You might want to rock her, and Timmy will want you to read him something." She shoves this little kid's story-book in my hands. "And don't shut the door all the way. He still wears diapers at night and he has an infection on his little you-know-what, so you might be aware of that while you're changing him," and on and on. She finally walked me into the kitchen while Timmy clung to her dress and whimpered. "You can fix him some sup-per—do you mind? There are hot dogs if you feel like heating them up—he likes them cut into little disk shapes."

I had completely tuned out by that time until her husband joined her in the lecture. "If he hits you, you should spank him. There's a pad-dle in our night table. He's not allowed to hit us. He knows what the stick means. If he doesn't come when you call him, you should spank him. He needs to know to obey."

Mrs. Piedmont handed Melody to me as they were about to leave. That was also the time when Melody decided to cry, of course.

"Oh—could you also bathe Timmy before bed? I really appreciate it, hon."

Little Timmy looked up at me with pleading eyes. "Don't beat me," his eyes seemed to say. I carried the baby around like a slippery squirming gift. I didn't know what to do with her. It was hard to play with the boy while the baby wailed so.

Timmy was sure it was my fault. "Why are you hurting my baby sister?" he asked, trying to pull her away.

I whisked Melody off to the kitchen. I opened

all the cabinets, refrigerator, and freezer. These people had absolutely no snacks, no "help yourself" food. I gave Melody her first bottle of the evening. I shoved it between her tiny teeth and grimacing mouth and picked up the phone to call Sonia.

I dialed the familiar number and waited for an answer. I suddenly realized there was a good chance that Jim could answer. Then what would I say? "Hi, I'm here with a screaming baby and wondered what you were doing for fun?"

Sonia picked up. "Sonia? Hi, it's Holly. Whatcha' doing?"

"Just getting ready to go out to a movie. Where are you?" she asked.

"I'm baby-sitting. I was just calling to see, uh, if you wanted to keep me company . . . Is Jim there? I mean, I don't want to talk to him, I just . . . is he home?" I stumbled.

"Yeah, he's right here making faces at me. Umm, Holly I'm sorry, I gotta leave. Do you still need help with your party?"

"Sure. Wait—how do you get a baby to stop crying? I'm serious. I'm like really sick of this." I was still picturing Jim sitting there at the kitchen table in his letterman's jacket laughing at me while I suffered.

Sonia told me to give the baby another bottle and put her to bed. So that's what I did for about two hours. I think she had a total of three bottles. I'd give her a bottle, march her down the hall to her room, and set her down writhing and red-faced in her crib. I'd wait, turn her light off, and shut the door at the very second I thought she was quiet. Then I'd step carefully before I heard her again.

When the Piedmonts came home I was asleep on their couch. It wasn't even that late, but there I was, spread all over their couch and drooling on one of their throw pillows. I looked up and there was Mr. Piedmont leaning over me saying, "Holly, we're home" over and over until I lurched and gasped awake.

I sat on their couch in a trance, embarrassed for sleeping and for wrapping myself in their afghan. Mrs. Piedmont came into the room carrying Melody, who looked exhausted, but she wasn't crying. Just as she lifted the baby to her shoulder the baby spit up all three bottles in a gush all over her mother's sweater. That seemed to be the appropriate time for Mr. Piedmont to drive me home.

CHAPTER

Sonia

I'm the new press secretary on my brother's life. I'm so sick of being in the middle, and I don't even like my brother that much. Not anymore anyway. I remember how I used to idolize him before I got to high school. He'd tell me all about school and try to impress me with all the activities he was into. Then he got a girlfriend and he'd ask me all this stuff about what girls are like. I felt like I was already part of the "in" crowd. I watched Jim at all his football games, and it never seemed to bother me when my parents gave him all the attention.

Well, it bothers me now. I don't want to live through another person's life. I want to talk about *me*. I want to have something to talk about. All Holly wants to talk about is Jim. I'm her therapist now. She should know what Jim's like at home these days. I sure wish I knew what his deal was. His new thing is to come home right after we've finished dinner. The other night was really bad. I wasn't surviving dinner real well. The conversation, once again, was Jim's absence and what did I know about it. Oh, and turkey. Turkey was the trigger for all kinds of stored-up feelings. Mom brings out this big plate of turkey like it's Thanksgiving or something and I try to contain myself.

"Would you mind if I just had a salad?" I ask humbly.

"Since when do you not eat what I make?" Mom says.

"I'm just not in a turkey mood."

Mom surveys the table and Jim's empty place and sighs. "There seems to be an awful lot of food for three."

I can't help it. My mother doesn't have to feed the pilgrims every single night.

"Your mother went to a lot of trouble to make this meal, Sonia. I think the least you could do is eat it and appreciate what's in front of you," Dad says.

Then Mom starts to cry and I'm left there without Jim to chime in or roll his eyes at me. It was all his fault, really.

"Jim doesn't come home for dinner and now you. Do you have to make it more difficult?" Mom whimpers.

"It's not my fault Jim isn't home."

"You worry about your *own* attitude," Dad says.

I couldn't wait for Jim to get home so I could tell him what a creep he was for playing invisible and leaving me to cover for him. I feel guilty, but in a way I was almost glad he was slipping up a little. Maybe now Mom and Dad would see he wasn't perfect. Finally the spotlight shifts and it's my turn to find out what life is like out there.

Jim lets the screen door slam, which Dad hates. He takes his time coming in, then hangs around the archway like he's just dropping in to see how we are. He has some serious nerve, I'm telling you.

"Hey, do we have any of those Little Debbie peanut butter bars? I'm starved." He looks like a pitiful bum.

"Jim, I would suggest you sit down and join us in a real meal," Dad says, pulling out a chair.

"Oh, really, I would, but all I really want is one of those peanut butter things, that's all."

I try to toss him one of those "Skip it you pig" looks, but he's clearly avoiding any eye contact with me so he can continue the big fake-out.

Mom is trying not to let Jim get her upset. "Another late practice, Jim?" she asks, like a mom from television.

"Yeah, we're getting quite a workout every day."

This gives me a sweet opportunity to excuse myself. The turkey episode is dropped into Jim's hands now. I'm not about to help him out of this one, and Dad is just starting to ask, "What is with our family these days?"

I'm sitting at this enormous table of cookies,

brownies, cupcakes, and cheerleaders who claim they never touch sweets. I know this is a lie because half the girls I know are professional bingers who have their fingers down their throats after lunch. I can't pretend not to like food. I eat more than I sell at these bake sales, and I love bake sales. It's my chance to be seen with the most visible girls of the school. It's like I'm invited to be part of them because I'm helping their cause raise money.

There's this one girl, Jaqi. She spells her name with a Q. She's always nice even when she's with the group. She has these way-long artificial nails she wears and paints bright red. Whenever she talks she spreads her fingers out like claws and admires them or examines them for chips. They always look freshly glazed. She definitely knows what it means to be sexy, and today she gave me a few tips that I think will change my present life as a nun.

I asked her if she's going to Holly's party this weekend.

"I'm afraid I've already made plans," she says casually in her scratchy voice. "Rick and I are going away for the weekend to his parents' place up north."

I've heard about Jaqi through all kinds of stories about her floating around. The most recent legend is not only has she slept with most of the football team, but she and her boyfriend Rick were found sleeping one morning on front campus under a blanket keeping warm. If there's anyone who knows about getting a guy, it's Jaqi.

"Would you ever ask a guy out on a date? There's this guy I'm pretty wild about, and I'm like dying to get to know him," I say, as if he's one of many.

"Sure, I'd ask a guy out if I really liked him," Jaqi says, acting sort of surprised but flattered. "Guys like that. They like a woman who's in control and can go after what she wants. I know that's what turns Rick on. I set up these little rendezvous where we meet and can be alone. It's great." Jaqi took her finger and ran it along the frosting on a nearby brownie. She was an absolutely naughty girl and loved it.

"Don't tell me—you're a virgin, right?" she giggled.

"Me? Well, yeah, sort of."

"Sort of? You either are or you're not. It's not such a big deal. How else do you show a guy you really like him?" Jaqi said. Coming from her it sounded so predictable, but it was like she was speaking for every girl my age who should know anything about guys.

I'd never done anything like arranging to get alone with a guy. My experience was still limited to the few times in junior high when I'd been sloppily kissed by a clumsy boy named Roger on a weekend band trip, and once in science lab after school with this boy Tim who I'd been told all day was going to kiss me. Thinking about it made me queasy, not like my feeling for Keeler—out of breath, stomach-in-my-shoes.

I smiled, thinking about me with the house to myself inviting Keeler over for a drink, then a smooth evening with the lights turned down. It would be just like TV. I would be someone he'd never imagined me to be, an irresistible woman longing to be discovered. There had to be some night when Mom and Dad would be out late. Jim was always out, so that wouldn't be a problem. The problem would be getting Keeler away from Jim!

"Earth to Sonia, come in?"

It was Holly. "Girl, you look like you're in la-la land. Are you OK?"

"Oh, yeah. I'm fine. But how are you?" Holly and I always had this fake language we used around her friends, like so they wouldn't know how things really were with Holly. She wouldn't want them to see she was dumped or anything.

"Do you think you and Jim will ever get back together?" I ask.

Quickly she puts the blame on him. "I don't know what's best. I think Jim's trying to prove something right now, but I can't ignore the way he's been acting."

I suddenly remember my parents are going to be out Halloween night, the night of Holly's party. Oh, perfect. The reality of my plan scares me a little, maybe because I want it so badly to work. I barely listen to Holly, who's rambling on about her party, about pumpkins and candy corn or something. Her voice fades out, drifts away, and attaches itself to the group of cheerleaders, who are no more interested in pumpkins than I am.

CHAPTER

Jim

I'm an open-minded plastic bag ready to explode. POW! Another football practice and I simply don't care. I'm suiting up in my stupid uniform for the millionth time and it doesn't seem to matter.

I remember one time when my mom was talking all earnestly about drugs. "Kids, just please promise me that you will never touch drugs, OK?" And just like an angel-faced choirboy I said, "Oh, no, Mom, I promise. You couldn't pay me to touch the stuff." Like a slow-motion flashback I hear my words over and over. And I meant it then. Drugs to us kids were things that "bad people" or "hippies" did. "And they don't love Jesus. Right, Mom?"

Well, yesterday I did some. Pot, that is. I needed relief, so I turned to Keeler. Seems like he's the one I think of lately because he's so mellow, a nice distraction, a little out of reality.

Or maybe he's more in reality than I am. I found him by accident, really. I was cruisin' past the park and I saw him at a picnic table leaning way over. "Hey, punk, watcha think y're doin'?" I yelled, scaring the life out of him. He jumped. "Jimbo, Man, get out'a here. I mean, get over here." I parked the car on the gravel and tromped across the grass. At first I thought he was just smoking a cigarette, but then I saw it was a tiny joint.

"Join me in some of Colombia's finest?" he asked slowly.

"Oh, no thanks, pal, I don't do that heavy stuff," I said confidently.

"Oh, sure. I forgot. You're a stud," he laughed. He took a long drag and looked at me. "You sure? I mean, don't take this personally, but you look awfully serious. You could stand to relax. Time out. Lots-o-time. No time . . ."

"Well, maybe a little hit. I don't know. I can't see how I can feel any worse about life now anyway."

"What's the matter? Lost your little Love Biscuit?" He was already rolling me one with careful accuracy.

"Basically. Holly and I just don't agree on life anymore." Keeler handed me my joint. I felt terribly foolish and already guilty.

"Now, don't smoke it like a cigarette. You have to pinch it tight and suck it in real tight. Hold it so it'll work. Right? And save some for me. The thing is I don't think you'll get buzzed the first time. I don't know."

I only had a few drags, but I felt kind of sick. I was waiting for this totally faraway trip out of my misery, but it didn't really happen. I felt a little like puking.

"So? Are you high?" mocked Keeler.

"I don't know. I'll have to do some more later."

"Do you mind leaving, Stanley? I need to do some drug shopping and like my Avon lady is right over there in that Volkswagen. Am I rude or what? But look. I'm here every day around this time, so look me up."

"Cool," I said quickly, fading fast. I was sure I was being followed home by the police. I was definitely late for dinner. My face was buzzing a thousand tiny vibrations, all the funny cartoon molecules having a party.

I came home and stood in the kitchen without any sense of wrong. I only knew I wanted something chocolate and would have to lie about where I had been.

The next day in the locker room I see Zyder looking over at me. He's got all his scamming friends around him, and I'm sure I hear Holly's name. It would be just my luck to lose her to a guy like him. They know they've upset me now and I catch one more phrase. ". . . everlasting legs." I slam my locker shut and glare their way. I think of Holly's little speech about us being too physical and her condescending tone about how every guy has one thing on his mind. She can't fool me. She's a tease. I want to blame her for the way the guys are talking.

Out on the field I feel like jello. I am numb. Coach adds to my hostility. I feel like he's judging every move I make. We run through some passes, a blocking drill. I am moving through the air around me like it was closing in. There's something I want to fight off. Every man in the defensive line is an obstacle. The quarterback throws me the ball. Robotically I go out for it, make the catch, but can't get past the defensive back. I'm running up against walls today. There's my parents. Boom! There's Holly. Boom! And they're all in the way of my freedom to run. They won't let me try out who I am. I can't take off.

Steve notices my bad mood as I get back in line.

"Your concentration's off. Something happened between you and Holly, didn't it?" he says.

"How'd you know?" I ask.

Steve's a little nosy, but at least someone bothers to care, even though he couldn't possibly understand.

"Well, I saw her get a ride home from Debbie the other night."

"I don't know, Steve. Things aren't working out right now."

Steve looks surprised. He must think I'm in trouble too.

The coach shows no mercy today. He calls us girls and blows the whistle. It's time for a scrimmage. I'm not the athlete I used to be. My mind's not on this game at all. It's on a tall, cold beer. Then I remember the scare I had after dinner last night when Dad called me out to the garage.

"Know anything about these beer bottles,

son?" He was standing over the plastic garbage cans dangling two Heinekens like they were dead fish.

"Uh, no, Dad, I mean, they're not mine if that's what you mean. I picked them up in our yard. The neighbors must be partying again. Keep America beautiful, you know," I laughed lightly.

He eyed me suspiciously and let the bottles drop. I breathed a sigh of relief and pretended to be interested in the chain on my bike. I was walking a dangerous line, drinking out on the driveway after Mom and Dad had started in on the ten o'clock news.

We're in formation. The quarterback calls the signal, gets the snap from the center, and fires the ball. I take two steps off the line, cross over the middle, and bam! I'm hit with the pass. At almost the same time I'm hit from behind and I fall hard. I hear the crunch as my shoulder is nailed into the ground. Then I feel the worst jab of pain right in the blade. I can't move. It hurts like a big dog. I'm rolling back and forth trying to be brave. Everything stops. Coach is there and all the guys looking down at me. Somehow they float me to the trainer's room. Out for the rest of the season for sure. My arm feels like it's holding on by a torn shoestring.

The trainer, Mr. Dobbs, is nice enough. Instead of talking about my injury he goes on about how well I played this season and how he's watched me improve. Why do I feel like this is a tribute to a player who's only history now? I start to pull my jersey over my head and wince.

"Uh, I can't quite lift my arm up, sir."

"Would you mind if we just cut the jersey off, Jim?" he asks quietly. This meant it was over for sure. I was shedding my jersey and any chance for future glory. I wanted to cry then. It was a sort of panic. It was like looking down at myself, feeling sorry for the pain and my loss of an identity.

Mr. Dobbs drove me to the hospital for X-rays, which showed that I had irritated my once-dislocated shoulder again. I was definitely out for the season, what little there was left of it. It was no big deal, but it *was* a big deal to me. This was my last year and I wanted to shine once more and at least get us to the championships.

Oh, well, what more could possibly happen? Could my life be any worse than it is now? The sharp twinges of white-hot pain were numbing now. I sat, bound like a mummy on the school steps, waiting for my dad. I was loaded on Demerol, almost asleep.

"Your shoulder again?" Dad asked.

"No, Dad, I'm wearing a shawl," I snarled. "I'm finished for the season."

"Oh, I'm sorry, Jim. Not fair, is it?" he said, leading me into the car.

"No, Dad, it's not fair. It reeks and I'm ticked off. Sorry. I'm just upset."

"I'm sure there will be more for you later this year, right? There's track?"

"I don't really care about anything right now, OK?"

I thought I heard him say he was proud of me. I don't know. I was thinking how Keeler might enjoy these Demerol pills. Maybe pot was helpful for pain. What was I, nuts? Was I some kind of wasteoid now that there were no sports to save myself for?

Anyway, after my Demerol had worn off later that night, I had this serious urge to party. I couldn't deal with this.

"You're injured, and you're still on that pain-killer, Jim. You are not going out," Mom said as I moved stiffly out the screen door.

"Mom, I'm not driving. I just need to go for a walk. I can't just sit around feeling bad for myself."

"All right, you win. But I will come looking for you if you're not home by eleven." Mom looked so trusting. She would be so hurt if she knew how many lies I was starting to tell. But what she doesn't know can't hurt her, I say.

Keeler

I'm like stoked. My dad and Judy finally decide I can come back in the house and live, but what does Dad do to me when I reenter the Emerald City? He has an important client over for dinner and makes me attend. I guess I wasn't exactly sure what it was my father did for a living until tonight. I found out he's in advertising.

I'm sitting in the living room alone with this guy my dad has over. He's a ferocious-looking dude with eyebrows that run straight across his face. I mean, it's a bushy highway. He's nervous, I can tell. He keeps clearing his throat with this slow 'a-hem.' Emphasis on the *hem*. I want to tell him to chill. My dad's game may be intimidation, but he's a mess during shows like "Little House on the Prairie."

My eyes are severely popping out of my face. I probably look like a pink-eyed rabbit. I quickly excuse myself for a drink of Visine in each twitching, begging eye. When I return, the man is staring at the cover of a magazine, holding it many different angles, and then nodding, for effect, no doubt. He seems like a fake from the start. The phony extra shake he gives my hand, the bold yellow tie and matching puff in his breast pocket. Fake.

"What does this picture say to you?" he asks, presenting me the magazine as if it were a plaque.

The picture shows a girl and a guy on their hands and knees in the sand. They're both in bathing suits wearing ridiculous grins. And let's just say the girl is very well stacked. I had no idea what this man was asking me to say.

I looked him straight in the eye, and in my most faggy voice I said, "Passion." Then I winked.

He sank deeper down into the couch. His face was tomato red.

"Uh . . . er . . . What we're trying to discover here is, uh, well, what sells. This magazine sells sporting and fishing equipment, and we wanted to represent playfulness and recreation. That's all."

"I'd buy anything from a babe with . . . well, we men aren't stupid—we know what appeals to us. Ha ha ha," I babbled. If my dad could hear me now he would just die. Serves him right, sticking me in here entertaining Mr. Recreation. Pervert.

"Have another cocktail wiener, sir?" I gushed.

"No, thanks. I'm fine."

"They're good . . . Liver paté perhaps?" I continued to annoy this man. He could always leave, which was what I was thinking about doing the moment Judy entered with the dinner.

Judy comes out of the kitchen with Dad following behind. He married her for her cooking. It was true my real mom couldn't cook anything that involved preparation, but at least she was real and could show some emotions. Judy looks like one of those cookbook models of the fifties in an A-line skirt with a platter of wholesome food.

"I see you've met our son," Dad says, looking a little nervous.

"Oh, yes, he's full of fun. You've got a lot to be proud of. There aren't too many youth today who have their heads on straight. My son got messed up in the drug scene when he was his age and, well, we've had a lot of heartache," the man said sadly. He saw right through me. Jerk. He was just trying to shove me for making him look stupid with the magazine. Dad looked at me with warning. I wanted to tell this man I had just finished a long, hard vacation in the car, thank you very much.

"Keeler, you *are* staying for dinner, aren't you?"

"Judy," I said, making sure to emphasize that I was using her first name, "would it be all right if I just went ahead and got started on my homework for tomorrow?"

"I suppose . . ." she started.

"Oh, good. Save me a plate—it looks delish'. It was a pleasure meeting you, Mr. uh . . . I'm sorry."

"Snodgrass," he said blankly.

"Sure." I took off out of there. I ran upstairs and burst out laughing. "Snodgrass! I'm so sure. Snot grass. Grass. Exactly. Scary how everything's connected."

I wasn't sure what I was about to do, but I knew I had to get out. I hadn't been in my room for so long. I bounced on my bed a little. I felt like I was in a hotel. Judy had tried fixing it up so that it looked like a magazine home or something. She claimed it was so she could "show" the house to her architect friends. She even had these stupid soaps and folded towels in my bathroom and this potpourri stuff that smelled like rotten peaches. I could definitely trash this room back to the way I had it. I wondered what she did with all the raunchy posters I used to have on the ceiling.

I opened the window and climbed out, swinging to the tree that always worked when I needed to escape. I slid down the trunk. When I got in the car, I cranked the stereo way up. I saw Dad and his guest through the window. Dad started to get up from the table. Then he sat back down. He and Judy had caught on. There was no way to control me.

I had to do a beer run. At least a six-pack. Consumption of the old hoochie-cooch and a baggie of grass would be enough for me tonight. I cruised through the quiet neighborhood, the route I knew so well, the trip to the park. So bourgeois. The tape I had in was so perfect. Words in the song yell stuff like, "Do you dare to stay with me tonight . . ." It was so on the edge.

There was this strange-looking night stalker shuffling along the sidewalk. He looked like a mummy, all bound up. It was Jim and he looked majorly despondent. I was more than happy to see him and had to catch myself from honking the horn like a goon. It seemed lately that he was appearing more frequently—a pleasant surprise. And it wasn't that I wanted to corrupt him or anything, I was just glad I had someone to hang out with who was a little more intelligent than the low life I usually partied with.

"You look a little injured, man. Or did they just let you out of security?"

"I got hit at practice today. Pretty ugly, aren't I. I feel like death, I really do. I was just going for the ball and I never saw him coming," Jim said.

"You really got nailed. Are you out for the season?"

He wasn't really listening. He wanted to rehearse his fall, like he had to prove to me that he wasn't normally weak.

"I've been hit harder before, but I was reaching and I fell wrong."

"Bummer."

We pulled into the park near my favorite place, where a statue of St. Francis of Assisi stands. There were many times when old Francis came in real handy for me, as I blubbered endlessly all the problems of someone who is stoned and can't put together the stupidity of life.

"Is this where you party? I mean, are there

cops at this time of night?" Jim asked suddenly.

"No problem, Jimbo. I know what I'm doing. Just don't start singing or disturbing any of the cosmos. Want a beer?"

"Yeah, thanks. Oh, I had some Demerol for the pain at the hospital," he bragged.

"Neat. My mom, I mean, Judy, my stepmother, takes Valium like candy. She's hardcore," I laughed.

"She's your *stepmother*?"

"Yeah, the wicked stepmother. Heh-heh-heh!"

Jim was downing the beers, I tell you. I hoped he wasn't a lightweight or anything, because I wasn't about to usher him home to Ma and Pa Peterson.

"Why does life have to reek?" he blurted between gulps.

"Oh, grasshopper, why does there have to be an answer? Shall we work on our debate theories now?" I asked, starting in on the baggie in my pocket.

"No, man, I'm serious here."

"Yeah, you look real serious. Sobriety . . . serious—schmerious. What do you want me to say? That your injury was God's will?"

"Easy," he said, doing a macho number.

"No, you were doing this religious thing the other day at the restaurant, so you must believe *something*."

"Well, yeah, I'm just used to knowing that there's a reason for things happening, like we're supposed to learn from things, whether they're good or bad," he said.

"Now don't get all confessional on me. You've had a few beers. See, I knew you were secretly a determinist because if you weren't, you would say 'Que serà, serà' like whatever happens, it'll work out. You can live with it. You can change it."

"Yeah, but why me? There was no way I could've avoided getting hit." I passed Jim a finely rolled joint. He was getting good at it now. Our breath froze in the chilly air. The smoke hung and fanned all around us. It was so sweet.

"So like you and Holly are history, huh?"

"Holly who? Christmas holly." Jim jumped. He was suddenly aware of St. Francis.

"Who's that over there?"

"Oh, the one with the hood and the little birdie on his finger?" I cackled. "That's St. Francis. He's watching you."

"I thought it was—Jesus, or a cop. Man, he's giving me the creeps." He passed me the joint again, smiling like a clown.

"You and Holly been going out a long time."

"Since sophomore year."

"You got in trouble for coming down on my side, huh?"

"It's not only that," Jim said.

"What then?"

"She thinks I've changed."

Sometimes Jim came up with the most up-tight statements, I swear. I wanted to know what it was like to have a conscience or whatever, and he was at least concerned about things being right or wrong. But then he was depressed tonight and I was . . . happy. *Happy?* What a stupid word. How about comfortable?

"How can you *not* change?"

"I don't know—what if you don't like who you are?"

"And who are you?" I kidded.

"I'm Liberace, who do you think?" Jim was cool, I decided. I knew that deep down he didn't want to give a rip. I wanted to change. I was bored with doing truckloads of pot a week. But what else was there?

"Let's go swing on the swings. It's awesome, man. You're already high, but you're like high, too, and you feel this incredible exhilaration. It's better than sex. Whoops! Sorry," I said.

"I can't swing in a sling," Jim laughed. "Sling-a-ling, hear them ring . . . ring-a-ling . . . in a sling."

I think that was the most fun I've had in a while. I was high and I wasn't alone. I drove Jim home at what I think could've been about two-thirty in the morning. His mom was peeking through the curtains when I drove up. I gave Jim a stick of mint gum and two drinks of Visine for each eye.

Holly

When you're a little kid the largest conflict on Halloween is your mom telling you that you have to wear a coat over your costume because it's raw and raining outside. This upsets you because you've taken such care to look like Raggedy Ann, a princess, or a clown, and it all seems like such a waste now that your costume has to be covered up by a stiff coat. The most people will see is your face. And, of course, it's always raining and wet on Halloween night, so that you come home with a sore throat and are warned not to eat the candy until Mom has checked it over for razor blades or tainted wrappers.

Now the conflicts are more adult. I've waited until the day of the party to make sure Mom and Dad will be gone for the night.

"Holly, I don't know what you have planned, but if we find there has been *any* alcohol here or kids up in the bedrooms, you will be *one very miserable girl,*" Mom says. Mom is making gallons of apple cider punch, cupcakes with pumpkin faces, and popcorn balls. This is turning out to be some little kids' trick or treat party.

"Mom, can I wear that flapper dress of yours, the one you wore for the Roaring Twenties party?" I ask sweetly. She's now stirring caramel for taffy apples. I wish she would just stop helping.

"That dress is awfully revealing. It's too low in the front. Why don't you wear a sweater set and be a fifties girl instead? I have a poodle skirt."

Terrific. A sweater. That's not what the other girls have in mind. I think Debbie's coming as a hula dancer in a little bandeau and Sandra's supposed to be a cave woman in a tiny bearskin.

"Is Jim coming tonight?" Mom asks. It's the dreaded question.

"Uh, I'm not quite sure—he may have other plans."

"Honey, you can tell me. What's wrong? You don't seem too excited about the party. I promise Dad and I won't embarrass you."

"I guess it is because of Jim. We're not getting along right now, and it's just not going to be the same without him tonight."

The phone rings and it's Debbie. She's hyper.

"Tonight's the big night, kid. Guess who's coming?" she squeals.

How did I know it was Chuck Zyder? This was the real reason I was nervous. I had this feeling the evening was going to be strange. I'd have to pretend to be having a good time, and I'd probably do the one thing I can't help. Flirting. Without Jim I flirt, and I'm just a little tease. And I'm spacey just like the rest of my friends. People just don't know how hard it is to be popular. You have to constantly think of ways to keep people's attention.

When Mom and Dad finally leave, I am overjoyed. I run to the stereo and turn it on loud. There are a few things I have to do yet. I cut up black garbage bags and drape them all around. They look like bats. I've decided to go for the flapper dress. Mom didn't say I *couldn't* wear it. She just said it was too revealing. I put on the dress and practice slinking around in it. The fringe shimmies as I dance. I love to get crazy. I don't think Jim has ever seen that about me. Maybe I can show Chuck the crazy me tonight.

I'm jumping around in my dress, eating trick-or-treat candy, when I hear a car drive up. It has the familiar sound of Jim's noisy muffler. I'd forgotten about Sonia, who was coming early to help me get ready. I didn't even have any makeup on yet. Holly the Halloween Hag.

My heart melts when I see Jim. I haven't seen him all week and I feel awkward. He's trying to avoid looking at me.

"Hi, Jim. How's your shoulder?" I see his face now—he looks terrible. He's pale, and there are dark circles around his eyes.

"Fine. I just can't play football," he grumbles. "We almost lost today with all the injuries."

"Yeah, I heard Reilly was out too."

Jim stops himself before he gets too chatty. It's like we're bad actors trying to act the emotion of resentment.

I give it one last try. "I'm sorry about the other day. I didn't mean to jump at you." There. That was sincere enough. And then suddenly I tell myself to forget Chuck. Start over with Jim. Start over with someone who really knows you.

"Don't worry about it," Jim says. "Look, I'll see you in school."

"Gee, isn't he a load of laughs?" I say after he's gone. "I guess he's not coming to the party, then, huh?" I had to make sure. If he was there, there would definitely be no love connection with Chuck, but then if Jim showed, how would I start things over with him?

Sonia looks good. She's wearing some southern belle number and for once looks like a girl. Or maybe she's Bo Peep. The afternoon is mellow. There's not much to do before the party. We act rude to the neighborhood children who come to our door for candy. They're like greedy sea gulls.

"Have you invited anyone special to the party tonight?" I ask Sonia. The first group of party guests has arrived. I'm seriously worried. They're the geeky type. Even their costumes are so typical: a greaser, a dog, and some giggly girl who's supposed to be a red crayon. They cluster around the refrigerator. The girl has already left a red smear on the wall where she's standing.

"Holly, I have a confession to make," Sonia says mischievously. "I invited your favorite ogre.

I didn't know at the time what it meant, so I told Keeler about the party."

Sonia! I could kill her! Obviously she likes this dweeb. I just don't need too many of the wrong kind of people here tonight. Someone like Keeler might ruin everything, or start a fight, maybe.

"I suppose it's all right. Maybe he won't even come. It's just that he makes me nervous. Everyone keeps telling me I owe him the benefit of the doubt."

"Maybe it's because he's so unpredictable. He scares me a little too," Sonia says.

I can't get over how pretty she looks. But why waste your looks on a loser like Keeler? Get real, girl.

More people are arriving. It's dark now and the room has a nice glow. The house smells like warm, spicy cider, and a hint of smoke that drifts in occasionally from the porch. Kids are polite enough to smoke outside. There should be no problems. I look nervously around for my group and any sign of Chuck. There's some commotion at the front door.

"R-O-W-D-I-E, that's the way you spell *rowdy*. Let's get rowdy! Woo!" It's Debbie and Sandra, who are clearly already a little drunk. They stumble in, hanging onto their dates, who are dressed alike in togas. I spot Chuck, who's casually strutting in behind them.

"Holly, hi. The place looks great. Are your parents gone? I'm a little wasted. Can you tell?" Sandra's falling out of her bandeau.

"You wouldn't mind if we brought a little

brew, would you?"

"Well . . . actually, I do mind," I start.

"Oktoberfest! Ya? Ve drink ze beer and get happy. Ya?"

Jeff laughs.

"Uh, you guys, I'm serious, OK? It's not that kind of party. No beer, really." My voice might as well be over a loudspeaker. I can't believe I'm actually speaking up for once.

"Is she for real?" Jeff is stunned, looking around for a reaction.

"Hey, chill, bud," a deep voice says. And then I see it's Chuck who's stepping in. His chest is clearly in Jeff's face.

They leave me and disappear to the driveway. Chuck has found me. I feel two hands on my bare shoulders. "Nice going," he says softly.

"Chuck, is that you? I didn't recognize you in your football uniform," I joke sarcastically. "What an original costume." I poke his hard chest with my finger. He's so tall and built. What a hunk. He makes me feel all petite and awestruck.

"Yeah, sometimes you just have to make do with what you have. I happened to have a football uniform. Those guys have some nerve, showing up at your party so trashed. I'm sorry they're my friends," he apologized. "Hey, do you want to take a walk or something?"

"Sure, I think the hostess should disappear for a while." I didn't see any harm in going for a simple walk with him.

He takes my little pinky finger and shyly leads me outside to my backyard, where a few

97

couples are already taking advantage of the harvest moon.

"So," he starts to laugh sheepishly. "Wow. You're just as gorgeous up close as you are from far away."

"Hmmm."

"You know, I've been checking you out for a long time. Even when you were with . . . ah . . . what's-his-name," he says.

"Jim," I say, rubbing my arms. I say his name out loud to remind him.

"Cold?" he asks, looking down at me.

"A little. Look, Chuck. I'm not sure Jim and I are officially over—yet . . . so maybe . . . we should just . . ."

"Get to know each other, right?" he grins slyly. I'm quickly stifled by Chuck's mouth, which has found mine, planting a long, hard kiss before I can move.

You . . . you don't get it, do you?" I gulp, pulling myself away before I can enjoy it.

"What? I thought you were—hey, look, forget it. But do yourself a favor next time and don't come on to someone if you're not serious." Chuck backs up, stunned, looks at me, and shakes his head.

There we stand and there is nothing I can say. I'm suddenly aware of the music coming from inside the house. The volume has gone up massively. I can hear the words of a moaning girl's voice singing: "I'm trying hard to read the signals. It's dangerous to watch your lips form words. Look at me, when I look at you. Take me somewhere, hey, I could really get to like this . . ." she hisses, along with a staccato accompaniment.

The noise from inside makes me anxious. Is this still *my* party? I feel stupid now that I have given Chuck the signals. But I'm finding out the hard way I can't continue existing to please people.

Chuck escorts me awkwardly inside. There is a crowd around the punch bowl. A group of burn-outs with leather jackets and ponytails stand there howling. Their ringleader seems to be some guy dressed like a mobster, and he's hovering over the punch bowl. I recognize the squinty eyes and machine-gun laugh. It's Keeler.

"What are *you* doing here?" I ask, parting my way between the stone cold stares of Keeler's crowd.

Keeler, chewing on a cigar, looks Chuck over, hesitates, and then asks me in a sweet voice, "Is, uh, Sonia here?"

Someone behind me says she went home.

"How about Jim, then?"

"Nope," Chuck grins. "Hey, you boys have a problem?"

"Yeah, this party is truly dead," complains one kid earnestly.

"Because the little hostess here wants to keep it clean," another kid laughs.

Chuck is getting rustled up. I don't want a fight. Not here.

"Maybe not all parties have to be gigantic beer bashes. Did it ever occur to you that some people can actually party sober and without recreational drugs?" Chuck says.

I want to hug him for sticking up for me like that.

"Dudes, let's get outta' here. Tony's having a huge kegger at his house even as we speak. We're wasting our time with these socialites." Keeler exits the party, his entourage following.

I'm highly relieved to have Keeler gone. His mere presence spells disaster. But soon the party seems more out of control than I can handle. Couples are parading upstairs for the use of the bedroom suites. I have no idea how to be a policeperson, but I have to do something fast.

Sandra and Debbie don't seem to care either. They think it's funny and keep saying, "It's going to hit the fan when your mom and dad come home. I was at this one party one time where the cops came. Yeah, it was really bad."

"Yeah, well, I'm not going to wait for it to get that bad, thank you. Are Jeff and Dave with that group out on the driveway in Cody's truck?"

"Yeah, why do you think we're sitting in here like old ladies? It's a guy thing or something. I love your outfit, by the way, Hol," Sandra says.

"Oh, thanks . . . Um," I say, taking a big breath, "I think I'm going to have to break up the party that's going on outside. And I have to do something about the couples upstairs."

"Holly, you're like a total wreck. Lighten up. Everyone's having a fabulous time. Don't be a poop," Debbie teases.

"Besides, if you break up the party out there, the guys'll want to leave, and if they bail out, so do we."

"Definitely," Debbie agrees. I look at these two and wonder why I've let them rule me all this time. I'm so sick of their games that suddenly the party that I gave basically for *them* doesn't mean that much anymore. And I know Coach will be stopping by sometime soon . . . not to mention my parents eventually. Not a pretty sight.

"Well, if you're not gonna' tell them their party's over, I will," I state firmly, waiting for a reaction.

Debbie and Sandra exchange knowing looks. "Fine. We'll tell them," Debbie announces, gathering up her hula skirt.

"You will? I mean, I know it's my party, but they're your boyfriends and I've already told them."

Sandra cuts me off before I can finish. She's truly mad. "No problem. Relax, OK? We're leaving. I hope you're happy now."

"Terrific party," Debbie hisses as she squeezes past me.

After they've gone I feel like I've been left in a snowdrift. There are still plenty of people inside having a good time, but I realize I haven't even tried to enjoy myself with them yet. I peek out the window in time to see "my crowd" hauling out into the night. I'm not sure how they'll treat me in school on Monday, but at least I know I did what I thought was right. I still have one more thing left to do before I can really enjoy what's left of the party. I climb the stairs and begin knocking on the bedroom doors.

Jim

I look at myself in the mirror. I look a million years old. I must have been quite the sight the other night when I got in late with Keeler. Dawn of the living dead. Mom was a phone call away from the police. I walked in very cautiously, like I was sober. Dad's face was taut. He had his coat on over his pajamas like he was about to go out.

"We'd like an explanation. If you're capable," he says, waiting.

I'm concentrating on the paneling of our walls. There was always this one spot where I could find a swirl that looked like a lion. It wasn't there now.

"I'm sorry," I say. Dumb. Very dumb.

"No, not just sorry. We want to know where you've *been* and what you've been *doing*. You have just about caused your mother a heart attack."

Come to think of it, Mom does look stressed out. I lean against the counter for support. How about the confessional approach? That you're sorry and didn't know what drinking could do?

"I was at a park with Keeler and we had a few beers. I really . . . I mean, I don't drink normally. I just thought I'd try it once. It's not for me. I mean, I'm not an alcoholic. I've tried it, and that's it."

They're not buying it. I'm not buying this story either. What if I told them about the pot? Would they freak or what? All I want to do is crash right now. Suddenly I feel this sadness rising in my throat. My lips start to tremble. I can't remember the last time I cried. I'm sputtering and wiping my eyes, trying to press back the tears. I'm a mess. I choke, and my nose drips all over. Is this an act too, or am I for real?

"Jim, is there something you're not telling us? Are you crying because you're sorry, or are you just—drunk?" My mom looks at me like I'm a stranger.

"No. I . . . could we just discuss it later? I told you what I did, and I'm sorry. Can't you see? I'm a little messed up."

"We realize you've had a tough day, but that doesn't excuse your behavior tonight." Dad pauses. "There are other ways to deal with disappointment. Have you tried telling God how you feel?" Dad asks quietly.

Sometimes I think my parents get all spiritual because that's the only way they know of to deal with heavy things. It's a safety thing.

Like they can't possibly fail if they use the Bible for advice. Why should I feel bad just because there's this sort of gap between us? This does not have to get spiritual. Keeler is probably sound asleep with no hassle from his parents. One of the few times I get toasted, and I have to get treated like the wayward son.

"I think you should spend some time thinking seriously about where this lifestyle might lead," Dad says. "Staying home from Holly's party and watching the house for vandals can be part of your punishment."

Mom says nothing; she only hugs her arms and looks injured. Her silence is punishment enough. I want her to at least ask me if my shoulder's any better. I want to hug her and push her away at the same time. She probably thinks I got exactly what I deserve.

Harsh. I'm lumped in a sling with snot running out of my face, and they're telling me I'm actually grounded. I haven't been grounded, I don't think, since I was about thirteen, when my best friend Teddy and I spray painted a four-letter word on the back of our toolshed. I didn't even know what the word meant.

That night I'm lying in my bed spinning. I can hear Mom and Dad saying their prayers. The whispers, sounds of s's, prayers said for me. Forgiveness for their son, who has tasted what it's like to be a little reckless.

Halloween night I completely blow off the punishment.

"By the way, Jim. No friends in the house, OK?"

"No problem, Dad."

I'm regarded as a criminal now but am allowed to drive Sonia to the party. She's unusually jolly in the car. She's actually a knockout. And Holly. Whoa! I may be a little mad at her still, but I'm not blind. She has a tiny bit of apology in her voice and a look on her face that wants me back. But I pull away, I might as well face the facts. I have to go my own way. I don't want to make the effort to get her approval anyway. Approval seems too tentative. You never know if you've done enough or been enough for someone. You slip a little, make a wrong move, let someone down, and they decide they don't trust you anymore. And how do you fix it once you've hurt someone? Like my parents, who see me differently now.

Two hours into the party, Sonia calls me. She makes me wonder when she volunteers to come home so I can be at the party—which is super nice of her. I mean, she knows I'm grounded, but somehow she has given me a decent reason to go. She says Holly needs to see me. Hey, when a girl needs to see you, you can't ignore it. I don't care how stupid I look. I *am* maybe a little bit—desperate?

Appropriately I show up at the party as a wounded army officer. The arm still in its sling. The first words I hear as I crawl through the crowd are, "Oh, my gosh, there he is." That right there makes me feel larger than life. It's Sandra, one of Holly's best friends. She's obviously out of it.

"Have you seen Holly?" I ask bluntly.

"Uh-huh, but you might not want to . . ."

"What do you mean? I heard she wants to see me."

"Wow, I'm like so confused," she rambles. The girl is tripping. I get this feeling of panic. Like Holly really could be a slut and I never knew it. But like that, would be totally not Holly's character. Man! And if *she* slips up, we're *all* basically lost.

I'm pretty impressed with the party, though. It seems to be going great. Lots of people have showed and I'm proud to be around them. I haven't been very social lately, I guess. It's good to be back in the land of the semiliving. Drugs can really bring a person down. But when I see Holly, she's like flirting with Chuck Zyder. I have to hold myself back from ripping him apart. Her face goes white. She already looks a little sick. He gets up from the couch slowly, slinks for the door, just leaves Holly like he was only visiting.

"I can explain, Jim. I was comforting him. He's depressed," she begs.

"I don't think so."

"You don't believe me? Look, Chuck asked me out tonight, OK? And I turned him down. I could've had something with him, but I didn't— and you know why? Because I still care about you. A lot."

"Hmm, that's too bad." I wasn't paying attention. "Do you want to talk? I came all this way . . ."

I continued to be cold. If I wanted to get anywhere, I'd have to forget I had just seen Holly with Chuck. It was just one more stab I couldn't think about.

"Here?" She asks. "We could go up in my room."

I'm suddenly overcome with shame, like she's too good for me. I want to ask her how she does it. How does she stay strong and true to her convictions? Like deciding not to dump me when she sees she easily could. What a princess she is. And this party is clearly happening—without alcoholic beverages, mind you. Somehow she just doesn't let people get to her.

So we're like actually sitting face to face on her bed with her bedroom door clearly open. She's sitting, or half-reclining, on one of her huge teddy bears. One that I won for her at a carnival. One that she'd soaked with my cologne, no doubt.

"This is so weird."

"I know, isn't it?" Holly shakes her head. "I kind of forgot why I'm mad at you."

"You're mad at me?" I'm defensive already.

"Well, weren't you sort of intentionally shutting me out? And I wasn't jealous of Keeler. I just saw that you were trying to act like him."

"Let's talk about us, not Keeler. I remember you said that you knew me better than anyone. I guess that bugged me because I all of a sudden felt trapped. It was like everyone was telling me who I was, and I didn't appreciate it."

"Can't you tell when people care about you? Sonia's concerned, your friends from the team don't see you anymore."

"If you cared, you wouldn't judge me. I don't

107

tell you all your faults." I was going to say more, but then I saw her dresser full of dried flowers, roses, and bouquets I had given her for proms and dates, and I decided it didn't matter, all this picky fighting. Why couldn't we just be friends?

"I think we've been too serious anyway. Maybe if we just go back to having fun together we wouldn't analyze everything to mean something else. I would like that," she says.

"Yeah, I would like it too. I'm too brain dead most of the time to notice stuff anyway. I mean, you know, with my injury I've just had a lot on my mind. I'll try and be more sensitive."

"Should we date other people?"

"Why—do you have someone in mind?" I'm sounding like a leech.

"No, but, if we're just . . . friends. Oh, I hate that phrase! Let's just not call it anything. We'll be ourselves and we'll see." She smiles at me for the first time in a long while.

"Yeah, nothing heavy. But can I at least have a hug?"

It's casual.

Sonia

Lying there in my bed I wondered. Maybe it was all a dream. Not that I hope it was, but if last night was real, why do I feel so empty now? Wouldn't the huge joy of it still be warming me? Keeler still seems near in the sweet smell of his cologne, the two of us in my little-girl room, pink and frilly with a few cute things hanging around.

Now I'm not a little girl anymore.

My planning had worked almost by accident. Mom and Dad gone, trading places with Jim, leaving for the party, probably just missing Keeler, who knew where to find me. I was secretly proud of myself for being such an actress.

Keeler was absolutely gorgeous when he showed up at the door. He was all dapper in a white suite and fedora. Any hesitation quickly left me. When I'm with Keeler I can let go of myself, act wild, be daring.

109

"Hi, Keeler!" I acted surprised to see him.

"Boy, you look nice tonight. Are you going out?" he asked.

"No, I just got back. Holly's party, remember?"

"Yeah, not much to remember."

I let him inside. He slipped by me, admiring the bag of candy. "Hmmm, let's see, do I want a trick or a treat?" He laughed, helping himself to a candy bar. "And a little kiss?" He leaned down and gave me a soft kiss. It was perfect.

My mind wanders back and forth between last night and now. When you want someone to want you and you don't want to lose him, you don't always analyze what you're doing. So you make the sacrifice and say goodbye to that prize called virginity you've tried so hard to defend. And it's almost like I have lost myself. He has a vulnerable part of me, and I'll never get it back. Somehow there should be a guarantee, now, that he'll still want me. We'll go out and it won't just be kid stuff anymore. It will really mean something.

Lying there in my bed my mind goes over what he said to me. "I wish we could stop time, freeze it right now with us here like this. Let all the days pass and just forget everything else. We could spend the rest of our lives together."

"Let's quit school, get married, and drive around the country in a van or something," I laughed, delighted at the idea.

"Yeah, we could like start our own commune," Keeler said.

"We could have a million kids and name

110

them exotic names like Asia and Zephyr. I could set up art shows while we travel all over the country . . . You could be in a band, maybe. Yeah!"

There were rock videos on television. I was sitting on the couch and he was on the floor. He had taken off his hat and jacket. I noticed how broad his shoulders looked under his shirt.

"Want me to give you a backrub?" I said, touching his back gingerly.

"Oh, that would be awesome," he said, sliding his frame up against the couch between my feet.

A sexy scene came on the video. A sultry girl strutted around, seducing the camera. A circle of men surrounded her, reaching out for her attention. Another scene came on. We sat comatose in front of the screen, taking it all in.

Keeler removed his shirt. "Come sit down here, Baby Blue," Keeler said, smoothing my leg.

I slid off the couch and plunked down beside him. The video was making me nervous.

"What's wrong?" he asked. "Are you afraid of me?"

"No, I just, I wish I wasn't worried about my parents coming home."

"Hmmm, that's a drag. Hey, I won't stay long. You know, I've been waiting to be alone with you for a long time." He began kissing me.

"I don't want to pressure you . . ." he whispered.

"Don't talk. This is nice."

You just don't think it will happen. But they

111

always make it look so easy on TV and in the movies. When you're going at it, you don't want to pull apart and say, "Halt!"

"You're such a kitten," he told me. "A wild one, I could tell when I first met you." We were really close now. My eye fell on the family portrait above the piano. The happy family. Me with glasses.

"Am I . . . wild?" I whispered. "I mean, I'll bet you've known a lot of other girls who are much wilder than I am." My mind pictured tough gangs of girls in leather miniskirts.

"No, you're different. But I feel like I can be myself with you. You don't intimidate me . . . Want to fool around some more?"

I guess because I said Yes we went upstairs then. All the time I was listening for the rolling grind of the garage door opening. My mother's voice.

But now, lying here in my bed, it's just another Saturday morning with the smell of pancakes floating upstairs. I could be twelve years old, nervous about piano lessons. But did it mean anything? He had smoothed my hair and said I was his "silly girl." When I close my eyes I can picture his angel face. But then I close my eyes again and see the shame that comes over him. He realizes that we could definitely be caught.

It was over all of a sudden, "Uh, I should go. I thought I heard a car. Your dad would probably waste me if he found us like this. Are you OK? I don't want you to think this was just a one-time thing. I mean, you know . . . I care about you." He gave me a playful punch on the arm and a wink for a promise.

A tap at my bedroom door brings me back to reality again. This *is* Saturday morning, remember? I pull my sheets up around me suddenly. "You and Jim should really get started on the raking, Sonia. It's almost eleven o'clock."

I feel like I have to take a shower. So no one can tell. It was weird enough coming down the stairs last night fifteen minutes after Keeler had left. Me in my sweatpants like I had just been kicking back since the party.

But I don't want to take a shower this morning. I don't want to wash away the memory. Yet I do. I hate to think that I'm feeling any form of guilt.

I'm in the sea of leaves now, futile piles we've raked. The morning is clear blue, a backdrop for the gold and yellow trees in all their glory. It's the last fling of summer. The trees are losing their few clinging leaves. The death of leaves. Everything seems so mundane. Jim is his same self. I wish there was someone to tell.

Then the handsome prince drives up. Keeler! My heart pounds out of my throat. I make my face expressionless. I can't be beaming when he spots me. Is this supposed to be the "morning after" feeling? He glances over at me quickly. Our little secret.

He's here to pick up Jim? Well, what did I expect?

CHAPTER

18

Keeler

I call it doing color. Sonia says I'm wasting paint, but I say I'm learning about the color cycle. I pour a glob of green and swirl some yellow in. Chartreuse. I've gone through a full bottle of tempera paint now. I'm restless. Sonia is working quietly on her picture. This is one of the only places I'm comfortable with her. I don't want to be one of those couples who walk through the halls, hands in back pockets or wandering along belt loops. Public display of affection. Why do we have to call it anything? Swirl some more paint—blue and red, like a royal red heart, like blood through veins. My heart bleeds for you.

"Wanna do something this weekend?" she asks, in a faraway voice.

"I don't know," I say, barely audible, tipping the paper so that the paint runs in streams. I blow the paint into splatters, bursts of dark and light.

114

I realize I don't know Sonia. Not that I had to to go to bed with her, but she seems different. Breakable, like she expects me to stay around. Hey, nothing's permanent. What can I say? I make these connections, like with Jim, a guy who's truly cool, and then in one stupid mistake, like getting it on with his sister, I could completely lose his respect. I can see it now. No, this is definitely a stupid risk. What? Am I, the man without scruples, feeling a little nervous? Naah!

But touch me, and for a moment I'm putty. I will be whatever you want and I will forget any hang-up I might have about you. Even though you get on my nerves and under my skin, I can like you. How you make me feel.

"I missed you," she says softly.

"Yeah, me too. Come on. Let's get out of here." I think I might like to be with her again. We could go to the lake or maybe in my car. No, not a car, that's too cheap. She deserves more than that.

"I can't," she says. "How about tonight?" I'm suddenly part of a schedule.

"Can't. Tom's got my car," I say, which is true. He *did* want to borrow it some time this week. I draw away.

I have this technique I call "the knife." I learned it from this highly disturbed friend I had at my old school. His name was Jodi, and one day he was trying to describe to me how shallow he thought relationships were. He said he had this imaginary knife on a belt right on him so that whenever he felt someone getting too close or invading what he called his "sphere," he would reach for his friend the knife. He couldn't use it or actually stab anybody. He'd just "touch" it so he would know that he could keep people away if he needed to.

"Maybe tomorrow?" Sonia asks.

"Maybe, but I still got that humanities to work on."

Then she gets into this whole thing about, is this the way things are going to be with us, hard to get together and blah blah blah. She thinks it's because of Jim that we have to hide and keep our little attraction a secret. No kidding. I tell her the truth, that guys get protective of their little sisters. I know I didn't become Jim's friend to get to Sonia, though. It's only what people will think that I'm worried about. And Jim.

Sonia says she has something to show me. She's already shown me the hickey that's appeared on her neck. She's almost proud of it, I think. Wears it like a medal. She laughs that she didn't know I had such sharp teeth. This is all new to her.

What she shows me is rolled up neatly in her art locker. It's a charcoal drawing she has made for me. I try to act touched, but I'm not a very sentimental kinda guy. Besides that, the picture is of a male and female unicorn frolicking in a sunset. I can tell the female because she has some sort of flower wreath around her neck. There are few things I hate more than unicorns.

I could play pinball for hours. Pull back, the ball snaps into play. Then *boing*! bump! score!

The ball is bantered by whatever it hits, no mind of its own. One ricochet after another. It's all chance. I rock the table a little, try and tilt. Like me, you set me off, say the wrong thing, and I'm gone, rolling to score or to fall down a hole.

I've called Jim for emergency reasons today. He's smoked me out of hospitality, and I am going to have to start selling instead of sharing. He looks dumbfounded when I ask him for a little money.

"Well, do you think you're interested in buying regularly or what?" I try to still sound friendly about it.

"Sure, no problem. Like, how much does a bag cost?" he asks innocently.

"An ounce costs about forty-five bucks," I say. "Maybe a discount for a friend." I feel edgy. He hasn't mentioned me crashing his girlfriend's party yet, or violating his sister, either, for that matter. Violate. Like it's a traffic violation. Oh, and will there be a fine for that? Jim is playing a wicked game of pinball. Seems like that's all he has left to do. What can you be when you're an ex-jock?

"I can have the ounce by Wednesday, man."

"Cool! Hey, free ball," he says. He seems to deny the heaviness of this business transaction.

"Oh, man. Never play a guy for money on his home table."

I decide to test him out on the range of Sonia's dating experience. Maybe he knows about the other night.

"Hey, does Sonia date much?" I ask.

"Not much yet. She wants to, though. You should've seen her last night," he brags. (Ooh, scared o' that one.)

Lucky me. Maybe I can keep this up after all, at least to convince myself that I can actually get close to someone without using them.

I concentrate on the music of the pinball machine. The chimes and blinking lights, *ching, ching, ching!* rattle in my brain like so many loose thoughts trying to come out. I look at Jim, and for a second I see the old Jim I remember from humanities that first day. It's the Jim who seemed so dogmatic and a little sheltered. Yeah, I'm sure that the old Jim would be ready to pound me if I were to mention anything about his sister. No doubt.

CHAPTER

19

Sonia

It's hard to describe. It's like there's a little man in my head or my brain's sitting on a teeter-totter or on a lever that presses down hard on my thoughts, making them extremely sad. Or there's a heavy blanket that's smothering my feelings. Depression. I've never really been depressed like this. I could never understand people who've described depression before. I figure, hey, you get sad, and you get over it.

Maybe it's the weather. November is the final letting go. It's the definite approach of winter and death, with no hope for any more warm and golden days. All the trees are naked and ashamed in their new state of disarray. Every day has literal gray skies with bruised clouds that suggest a soon flurry of snow. The trees are the saddest, though. They're gray skeletons with spindly arms.

Today is raw and damp. I think of a reason

for my blues. Or grays. PMS. That's what my mom always explains it to be. Where everything seems hopeless and colored by those strange hormones. But I'm waiting for the reliever, when my *M* will finally come on its cycle and bring me back to normal.

Keeler leaves a note stuck in my locker. It says: "Meet me at the band shelter. Keeler." I'm exhausted after running laps in gym class. My legs feel like they're going to fold, and I'm short of breath. I decide to meet him anyway. I walk slowly to the park, shuffling the moldy leaves along the curbs and kicking up locust pods that rattle with old seeds. Leave it to Keeler to be mysterious, yet he's not what I thought he was. I mean, he's not as romantic with me anymore as he was that one night.

As I approach the band shelter it starts to drizzle. I can't see Keeler anywhere. My heart sinks and I feel tearful again. Then I see him sitting up against one of the railings. He looks like a black ant in his jacket.

"Hi," I say. "What did you want?"

"You know what I want, little girl, heh-heh-heh," he snickers.

"Cut it out," I sputter. "I tramped through the drizzling rain here, so quit being a pervert."

"Whoa, take it easy. Sit down here and tell me what's up."

"I'm just sad today. Is that a crime?"

"Do you need a hug?"

"I guess." He pulls me against him. I squirm a little. His jacket, with all its zippers and pins, is sharp, though I like the smell of the leather, kind of wet from the rain.

We get up and walk toward the playground. There's a group of guys in the back of a pickup truck. The truck is part of a float for the big football game tomorrow night. They have a dummy of one of our football players tied to a stake ready to burn. I can feel them watching us.

"Klan meeting tonight, fellas?" Keeler says. "Where are your hoods?" I tell him to shut up. They're obviously from the rival team. We continue to walk on by as they spout different obscenities. Keeler takes my hand and crushes it. Could he be scared? I wonder.

A flock of geese approaches us as we cross a field. They look like they're stalking us. The whole field is littered with their remembrance. We step carefully like it's a mine-field. There's a dark feeling, like every step is closer to an explosion. One of the largest geese runs at us hissing. Keeler hisses back and makes me laugh. I laugh so hard, and then a panic comes over me. I can't stop laughing, and then there are tears coming out, but they're real tears. I can feel the shift to real sorrow. Something struck, something tapped. Get a hold of yourself. Breathe.

"Hey, are you crying for real?" Keeler laughs.

"I think so—I don't know," I say, laughing again, nervously. Everything has become bigger than life. The geese, the mean boys in the truck, and the awful rain that has become heavier now.

"Hey, get a grip. Should I like take you home

or—do you take pills for this?" he asks. I start up again, laughing this time, and then sobbing.

"Whoops. Sorry, I didn't mean to upset you. Sonia, do you want me to take you home?" He's gentle now, and kind.

"Yes, please," I stammer, embarrassed at all my makeup that's running and the blubbering I've done for no explained reason.

In the car I close my eyes and take deep breaths. I remember one time I hyperventilated, and got prickles up my arms, and my hands went into stiff claws. I thought I was possessed. I didn't want to experience that again. Just think peaceful thoughts. I whimper until I'm home. Keeler walks me to the door. He looks very concerned, almost responsible for whatever it is that's wrong with me.

I am lying in the dark of my room, curled into a ball. Very safe, I'm well aware of what time it is. It's six-thirty on a Friday night, the night of the big game and the bonfire. Even if we don't win, there will be lots of parties, big bashes at all the homes of team members. Even Jim, the "unsocial one," is going. I pretend I'm asleep when Jim knocks on my door. Hopefully no one will ask what's wrong. My heart aches when I hear the car's muffler chugging out of the driveway and down the street. Emotional over a muffler.

Mom made pizza tonight. The smell of it filled the entire house and made me absolutely ill. On my way to my room I began to heave, covering my mouth just in case. Now, as I lie here in bed, I continue to think about smoky smells, burning leaves, bonfires. The nausea rises in waves. I try to lie very still. This must be PMS, I think again. It's almost Thanksgiving now. This Thursday. Wow, where has the time gone? I seem to mark everything by the one major event of the fall—Keeler and me on Halloween night. The event that seemed so major then, but so stupid now. I actually believed he loved me that night, but since then I've waited for more to happen, and it never has.

Mom is standing outside my door. I can see her shadow in the hall light. "Sonia?" I make a small noise. "Honey? Are you sleeping, or are you just lying there in the dark?"

"I'm kinda sleeping," I moan.

She comes over and sits beside me on the bed. "This isn't like you. You're usually the first Pep Club member at these big games. Your father and I were thinking of going over there. Would you like to get dressed and come along?"

"I'm not really up to it."

"Don't be down, honey. Where do you feel sick?" she cooes, smoothing my hair. I remember all the times when I was sick in grade school when she would care for me. I almost enjoyed being sick then. But now I'm not really sick, I'm simply depressed.

"Is there anything I can get you?" she asks.

"I'll be OK." I assure her.

"Are you OK to leave home alone, then?"

"I'll be fine," I tell her again. I say this to convince myself.

Monday I'm semi back to normal again. I feel

left out, though, around my friends who are still talking about the huge victory our team had Friday night and about the parties that lasted until the next day. Why wasn't I there, they ask. Yeah, why *wasn't* I?

Jaqi still carries a buzz from the weekend. Her eyes, a bit glazed over, slice me when I tell her I was sick the night of the game. And speaking of sick, where is *M*? No reason I can't ask Jaqi her opinion on a missed *M*.

"Jaqi, have you ever been . . . late before?" I ask casually.

"Yeah, everyone has now and then. Why?" she answers, bored.

"Well, it's just that I've never missed it before. You know how it is."

Jaqi looks at me doubtfully. I trust her. I *am* trusting her. After all, she was the one who gave me the courage to make the first move with Keeler.

"Is there a reason to worry?" she prods.

It's hit me now. The thing I've been denying all along. It's the big *P*. She's guessed it, and now I have to admit it. This is the reason I've not been myself. This is what you get when you don't use protection, stupid! Yes, there is reason to worry. Definitely.

"How late are you, Sonia?" she asks, jolting me back into this conversation I've initiated. Shoot! Shoot! This is not happening.

How late are you? How late are you? How late? Too late. Too late to change it. She's waiting. I can brush it off. It's not like she hasn't faced this kind of fear before. Hey, I'm in her league now, the practicing nonvirgins.

"Maybe it's nothing," I mumble numbly. For that's what I am. Paralyzed. My nerves are frozen over. Late. Jaqi leaves me for her boyfriend. I wasn't about to confess to her anyway. So now what? Is *this* what I am? Pregnant . . . with child . . . in the family way . . . expecting . . . knocked up . . .

But wait. I review the calendar again. It's November 20. That means almost one month pregnant. But I can't be for sure until I take a test or see a doctor or . . . how do you take those tests, anyway? I have to find out for sure. Don't think about it. Don't think about it until you're totally sure. This is not how it's supposed to happen. It's supposed to be happy news. Happy news that you tell your mom over the phone and tell your husband over a romantic dinner. "We're going to be parents." No way. This can *not* be happening.

I walk through the halls, sure everyone must know by now. They can see it in the way I walk. My face looks different, expectant, probably. And then the terror. The slut of the school has my secret. Jaqi could tell a hoard of people before I've even found a drugstore that has a quickie preg test. Before the final bell of the day rings, I start to run out the double doors of school. I run until my head pounds and my side aches, and I can't remember why it is that I'm running.

Jim

I drop the bomb at dinner. I need cash badly, so I say I need money for some parts for my car. Dad waits, pinching his bread in midair, and analyzes the car first.

"I thought you had it running OK," he says.

"Well, I got it tuned up, but the starter's wearing out." I pass over it quickly so we can end this interrogation and get on with the money. Then Dad totally shocks me by offering his Visa card. Sure, Dad, I'll pay you back. Hey, Keeler, do you take credit cards, or can I charge it to my account?

Dad digs in his pocket for his wallet right there at the table and hands me the card, at the same time inserting a brief editorial on privileges and responsibility. Why is nothing free? There's always some obligation attached.

"Uh . . . thanks, I've been thinking about getting a job." Shoot. Now that I had Dad's Visa, there was no way I was going to use it to support my recent habit. I would definitely have to work for it.

The phone rings like it always does during dinner. It's Holly calling for Sonia. Right away I get the look of pity. Dad asks if there's something wrong between Holly and me. When I tell him we're seeing other people, he starts to trip about friends who I've stopped hanging out with. Whatever, I give up.

"Why don't I hear about Steve anymore? Is it just since you've been off the team that you don't get a chance to see him much?"

"I don't know."

"What about the Camfeld's boy, Dan? Now there's a good family. He seems like a nice kid. Have you ever met him, Jim?" Mom asks.

"No, Mom, I haven't."

Sonia escapes all forms of questioning. She cradles the phone to her shoulder and talks quietly with her back to us.

I'm not particularly jazzed with the topic of friends. In fact, in the words of my esteemed friend, Keeler, I'm feeling bellicose. I swear, his language is so choice sometimes. When I asked him what the word meant, he said, "Look it up, idiot." It means "eager to quarrel."

I calmly excuse myself, denying my parents the pleasure of a debate on bad influences. I can feel the topic wafting along in the wind. I address my parents like children, like they'll just have to accept my lifestyle and deal with it.

"Keeler's picking me up."

"I keep hearing about Keeler. When am I

going to get to meet him?" Mom asks innocently.

"Look, Mom. He's not your type," I kid, rapidly dismissing myself.

Mom gives me a giddy swat on the shoulder. Hopefully the record of my activities with Keeler has been erased. I touch the thin rectangular Visa card in my back pocket. Yeah, Keeler will really love this. A serious drug shopper.

My new boss's name is Hank. That's the first problem. He's mostly belt, like he wears his slacks too high, and the wasteband rides slightly above. His face is doughy and expressionless. During the interview he chain-smokes and glances over me through slit eyes.

"Can you push a vacuum?" His cigarette bounces on his lips.

"Sure. Yessir," I say, trying to take him seriously.

"Any history of drugs, theft, anything?"

"No." I wonder if he can detect anything on my breath. Where's the chewing gum when you need it?

My new position at Mathers, Kappelstein, Worthy & Griffith is now assistant janitor. I clean four floors of plush offices after six-o'clock; empty the trash if there is any, polish anything that looks dull, and dust over the desks if I can find them under all the papers and junk. That's what Hank says, anyway.

When he leaves I'm left with a vacuum and a cord that only reaches for a few feet. I'm strongly tempted to do this job stoned. There's a great stereo system throughout the offices. The bad news is it only plays this mushed-over music they play in the doctors' offices and supermarkets. I shudder when I hear a saccharine version of the Stones' tune, "I Can't Get No Satisfaction." Between vacuuming moments I pause for feelings of power in the big leather chairs behind the desks. I lean back, my feet up on a desk, and reach for the phone. I page different offices, listening to my muffled, nasal voice trapped inside the box. "Mr. Kappelstein, line 5. Mr. Kappelstein, line 5."

The thrill of managing my own office wears off quickly and soon becomes extremely mundane. I think I've picked the wrong job. It's the kind of job that doesn't give your brain anything to do. I'll have to bring my Walkman next time to drown out all my thoughts. I figure that my salary for one evening of vacuuming and bathroom cleaning will buy me a nice bag of pot. What a trip. I'll have to save some money for Christmas too. Knowing Mom and Dad, I'll have to give account for the money I've made. That's one thing that really bugs me. I'm getting talks on accountability. We're accountable to God, accountable to our parents. Like what we do will ultimately affect others. I've heard it all since I was an infant. I always have to answer to someone. I can't wait until I'm truly on my own so that I can do what I want with my life, with time, money.

It's another Thanksgiving and I'm full. Full of relatives, full of heinous amounts of food, and full of a lot of talk that makes me out to be more of a bumbling idiot than my family knows. We sit around an immense table that's covered with food, and it's the same old family roasts on each other. Families are the hardest groups to answer to. They're either the most critical or blind, accepting or unforgiving. All the same, the questions are relentless.

My Aunt Elaine grills me constantly. "What are your plans for the future?" "I don't remember your hair being so long last time." "How has your football season been?" I thought I could avoid the football question.

My Uncle Paul, my sports hero since age seven, apparently wasn't told I hadn't finished the season. Ever since I was little I've tried to excel in sports, and it wasn't for my dad as much as it was for my uncle. He'd been all-conference in high school and was all-American in college. He decided not to go pro, did some coaching on the side. Now he looks at me like I've blown all the dreams he had had for me. His disappointment reminds me I still feel something. All this time had gone by since the injury, and I had dulled the pain with partying. Without chemicals I was insecure and couldn't define who I was. I couldn't accept my loss in football and look forward to any future in other sports.

Now it is Sonia's turn for questions. Sonia has remained quiet all during dinner, shuffling her food around her plate and looking generally forlorn.

"Do you have a special young man in your

life, Sonia?" asks Aunt Elaine. She's one to talk, the unclaimed blessing of the family, who at age forty still believes God has someone for her.

Sonia looks up hostilely. I catch her eye, and she gives me a puzzled look like she's worried I'm going to make a smart comment.

"Sonia's after an older man these days," I say slyly.

She looks at me again with a strong look of warning and mixed hurt.

"Oh, really?" says Aunt Elaine. "They say that's the trend these days. So what's his name?"

I look around the table at my captive audience, then at Sonia, who's pleading with me to shut up.

"I don't have a boyfriend. Jim doesn't know what he's talking about," Sonia says with disgust. She actually looks like it matters to her. Like she might cry. Aunt Elaine lets it drop and begins picking on our cousins, which is a lot easier to handle.

After dessert I nicely suggest that we might all be dismissed. The football games are on TV, and I'd like to just lie around in the heaviness of my turkey dinner. Dad holds up the show with a devotional sort of thing where we go around the table and name one thing we can be thankful for. Dad surveys the family and proudly announces that he's thankful for a family that loves God and for his wife and two children, who also live their lives to please God. When the so-called microphone is passed to me, I'm still stunned by what Dad said about his Christian kids. It puts the pressure on.

What am I thankful for? What did I say last year? I probably had something touching to say. I'm totally blank. I go over the old blessing clichés. I can't truthfully say "my family" because, well, because Dad said that one and besides I don't feel like it. Last year I probably mentioned football, but that's out this year. Pass. So jokingly I say I'm glad to be almost out of high school and graduating—hopefully. I laugh and then add I'm glad the Lord saw me through. My words come out like they've been pasted on. An afterthought that wasn't originally intended. Like my relationship with God right now—something I'd rather think about later, something that's slipped so far I wonder if it's possible to get it back.

CHAPTER

Sonia

This little kit will either ruin my life or save it. I have to know for sure, or I think I'll crack up. This secret is killing me, like any second I could be found out, and I wouldn't even be prepared to explain how this happened. That it's all just a really sick joke that can be fixed, no problem.

I can't believe this is me. I was the one in the drugstore today, my heart pounding at the check-out counter with a silly pregnancy kit in my hand. Mom was only aisles away looking for mouthwash or nylons, and I was the adult buying this kit that I had no clue how to use.

In my dream the judge asks me if I understand how the kit works. I say No. He asks if I understand what to expect while I'm pregnant. Again I say No. "Well, do you at least know how you got that way?" Well, Yes, I do know that.

This is me, locked up in the bathroom with an entire laboratory that decides my future, and instructions that are as foreign to me as being pregnant. All these steps. Why can't someone just come bursting in here with the results and relieve me? I begin the test using the eye-dropper, drop one fluid into another. My entire universe falls into the sterile test tube. I can't take this suspense. Drop, drop. I let it stand for ten minutes like the directions say. I can't possibly leave the bathroom. I'm afraid to watch whatever it is that's supposed to happen in the test tube. Should I pray? Would God be on my side in a situation like this, or would He let me get what I deserve? It can't hurt to whisper prayers. Like magic.

"Let me not be, let me not be, let me be . . . let me be OK. Let me not be . . . let me not be . . . please. My parents, my school, my friends, people at church . . . Let me not be . . . I'm sorry, I'm sorry. Just let me not be. Please, please, please!

Add another solution now. Waiting is the awful punishment. OK, so what will I do if I *am*? What will I do? Time to dip the little magic stick that will tell me the facts. I dip it, swirl it around, and rinse it off. It's pink. What does that mean? It's a girl? No, wait, the directions say it means positive. Is positive good? Yes, because if it was negative that would be negative news, bad news, and positive is up, right?

There's no one to answer these horrible questions. I still have a tiny hope that I'm saved until I read the elementary key at the bottom of the page: "Positive indicates pregnancy. Negative indicates no pregnancy."

The awful truth is that I'm positively positive. That's it. I feel sick, another wave of nausea and panic. Where do I go? It's like a nightmare or a movie that you know will only get more horrifying and gross. You cover your eyes so you can't see. Or you shake yourself consciously in the dream so that you'll wake up before the bad guy gets you. Or those dreams I've had where my legs are stuck and I can't run fast enough for help. This can only get worse.

For the first time my body actually feels swollen. It's only a month, but when I look in the mirror, I look fat. I look at myself sideways. I'll have to wear big shirts and baggy pants until everyone knows. I can't hide up here forever. It's like the time I borrowed my mom's blouse and spilled nail polish on it. I rubbed it and rubbed it and tried everything to get it out, but it only got darker and more obvious. Who can I tell first so that when I'm found out the stain isn't so severe?

I put the test and all its equipment in a brown grocery bag and sneak it downstairs. I want to shatter the fragile tubes to a million pieces. Disposable. Like me. Luckily there's no one home tonight, or I would most likely burst the news out in a hysterical speech. I would be immediately sent off to a home for unwed mothers, taken away kicking and clawing by austere nuns in black robes.

Outside, snow is hovering. It's bitter cold, too cold for only December 1st. I put on a coat and walk around our block in a trance, not quite sure where I'm going or if I'm even safe. I move stiffly. There's this pain in my heart that wants to choke me.

How can I tell Keeler? I want to scream his name out into the night air and let it freeze there. I'm so ashamed. Most girls would've been smart enough to use protection, but not me! My first time, and I'm pregnant. How will *he* be able to help me? I don't love him. I don't feel anything but repulsion for him now, but his baby's inside me. I wish I was dead. I pick up a shriveled leaf and twirl it between my two fingers. Its color is gone. Its life is over.

My thoughts are scaring me. I have to call Keeler. I have to know that I can tell him soon. I need to get this over with. I call him from a pay phone at a gas station at least a mile from our house. I've never called him at home. He sounds aggravated. It's like getting through to a wall.

"Keeler, I need to see you tomorrow." My voice comes out fragmented and unsure.

"Yeah, OK, where?"

"Wherever. The mall? The mall at . . . noon?"

"OK, I'll be there." He hangs up. I'm relieved, since there's nothing more to say. I'm afraid if I start talking, the news might spill out before I'm prepared.

I wait for Keeler on a bench in the mall. I'm guarded, ready to state the facts without any emotion. I don't want to be the sniveling girl who got herself in trouble and needs help.

Tinny Christmas music plays over loud-speakers. "He's making a list . . . checking it twice, gonna find out who's naughty or nice . . ." The words mock me like a scolding. What a pathetic place to announce you're pregnant. Mothers lead around whining kids who display ugly tantrums over toys they can't have yet. Everything has to do with being a mother. Come on, Keeler, be easy on me. Understand me.

Keeler appears like a ghost, smoking a cigarette. He's impatient and uneasy. He stands rigidly against a wall, waiting on me to say what I have to say so he can leave.

"I didn't think you'd come," I say. I'm still thinking.

"Of course I came. But why were you so mysterious on the phone?"

I begin my speech, swallowing a few times, praying for courage.

"After Halloween, I missed my period. When I was seven days late, I got a home pregnancy test. It came up positive." I emphasized the weight of the word *positive*. Maybe he wouldn't understand it either.

"Are you sure?" he asks, irritated. "Sonia, you didn't use any protection?" he reminds me in disbelief. "Gee!" he mutters.

"Keeler, it was the first time, and no, *we* didn't," I confess.

"I don't think you should rely on those tests," he says stolidly.

All at once my words come in a fury. I want to rip him apart, have him feel what it feels like to have this. How can he be so insensitive? Nothing shakes him, not even something like this.

"You jerk! I've been living with this since Halloween. I can feel what's happening with my body. I wouldn't have called if I wasn't sure!"

Keeler is stunned for a moment. My tears are very close. I have to be strong. I don't want pity. I want answers. Keeler comes over and sits down beside me, but he holds back from getting too close. "I'm sorry," he pauses. "But what can I do?" he says—earnestly, almost. And I almost believe he means it. And sorry is almost enough.

"Nothing. It's already been done," I say, realizing the tragic fact in that.

"Well, we have to do something. Have you thought about an abortion?"

"I've thought about everything. Over and over." I drift off. My head hurts from thinking. For all I know Keeler could have left me by now. He's entirely detached, it seems, from my little problem.

"Well, we can't get married. That's out, you understand, don't you? I mean, I thought I loved—er, liked you, right?"

"Right, I know. I feel the same way. About marriage," I mumble.

"You could give it away . . . Oh, man, this is rough." Keeler sounds like a little kid, like, "What do you want to do? I dunno, whatta you want to do . . . I don't care . . . doesn't make any difference to me . . ."

"Look," he says, "if you want, I'll give you some money for an abortion. That way you won't have to go through any more than you already have. You haven't told your parents yet, have you?" he asks.

"No, I haven't. But I don't think I want an abortion, Keeler."

"I'm just saying you can eliminate a lot of unnecessary hassle by doing it that way. I mean you've got school, and, oh man, this is such a bummer." He pauses. "Hey, do what's best for you. That's all that matters."

I wanted to say, Thanks for nothing, Keeler. Why did I even think he could help me figure things out? According to him, it's easy. Just get an abortion. It's my problem. Why does he even have to be involved?

He sat there for another moment until the tension between us got really uncomfortable. I was sending him signals to leave. His cigarette was making me sick. I didn't care if I never saw him again.

"I don't know, Sonia. I need some time." He got up suddenly without looking back at me and was gone. I thought I saw him disappear into the video arcade.

It was like I had been punched in the stomach. He had bunched me with all the other girls my age, younger, older, who chose to erase the mistake with an abortion. The thought of it started me shaking. I pictured me on a cold table, feet in the stirrups, screaming for my mother, while some doctor with beady eyes and sharp instruments vacuums me inside out.

"There. It's over with. It's gone." Like a sore tooth. There's only a dull throbbing left where a life could've been.

I remember a time when I was at the carnival

139

with my aunt. We rode the tilt-a-whirl until we thought we would pass out. The ride operator let everyone off one at a time but continued to pass us by, leaving us dangling upside down at the very top. I could almost hear him cackling at his own cruel trick from down below. We screamed and hollered every possible threat, but it only made him crazier. The ride started up again with a jolt, more violent and twisting than the first time. I screamed until I was hoarse and clung to my aunt. Any time I opened my eyes the treetops would blur by and turn to black. When he finally did let us down, we could barely walk.

I wander through the mall. What's next? Can I get off the ride yet? I think about going home, then think again. I can't risk meeting anyone here in the mall. I stick to store windows, looking at mannequins with wan smiles and one of a swiveling Santa. I look at Santa and think, "a belly that shook like a bowl full of jelly." My stomach can't possibly get that big. I'm too small.

Just then I hear a familiar voice behind me. It's soft and sleek like Holly's. She *would* have to be part of the drama!

"Sonia, how've you been? I haven't seen you for a while."

My first impulse is to zip up my coat or just run off, but she seems so welcome after my time with Keeler that I could easily turn to her for help. She invites me to go get a Coke with her. I want to latch on to her right there, tell her everything, but I'm timid.

As she sits down I find myself unloading everything. I tell her about the night of the Halloween party, how I planned it to go that way, how Keeler had almost placed a spell on me ever since I met him.

Holly looks confused, or just incredulous. "You don't mean you and Keeler—did it? Oh, my God," she gasps. "I can't believe this. Keeler? That's so stupid!"

Right there I fold. All the tears I was holding in burst. She doesn't give me a chance. Can't she see I'm crushed?

"Who else knows?" she marvels.

"Only Keeler. He was just here."

"What'd he say when you told him?"

"Nothing, really. What could he say? I'm pregnant, Holly. There's no way out. I don't even know why I talked to him."

Holly's more worried right now about who knows. And it's probably not as much about my reputation as it is for hers, knowing her. What if she was seen befriending a sleaze who got herself in trouble? Well, that would just ruin her image as the chaste and hard-to-get one.

"You're so smart," I blurted. "Why don't you tell me what I'm supposed to do? Keeler thinks I should get an abortion."

"Are you kidding? How can you even *think* about that as an option?"

"What am I supposed to do? Have it at fifteen? With no father? I wish I could say that I loved him, or that there was even a chance we might get married after this, but there's just no way."

141

Holly has nothing to say to this. She gives me a quick pat on the hand, all flustered, and quickly leaves me with nothing resolved, and feeling worse than I had after Keeler.

I keep my head down and slink past staring people to a bathroom. If I can just make it home now, I don't care. If I don't collapse right here. I fumble for a bus token and clutch a wad of tissues. I press my hot face to the bus window on the way home and pinch myself to keep from crying.

CHAPTER

22

Sonia

Now the only place to go is home. I'm so broken and shaky, all I need right now is for someone to be gentle, to make it better just for a few minutes. Someone to smooth my head and tuck me into bed.

Mom sits at the table patiently cutting up vegetables. She's contained, perfectly content sitting there in her own domestic world. The kitchen is quiet except for the hum of the refrigerator and the congested hissing of the dishwasher.

Mom takes one look at me and immediately knows I'm upset. I stand there hanging my head, sobbing. I clench the tissues in my fists, trying to brace myself against the steady hurt.

"Honey, honey, what is it, Sonia?"

"I, I . . . ohhhh!" I can't get the words out. If she'll just hold me, I'll be all right.

Mom encloses me in her arms and rocks me

back and forth. We're a single island, safe, a circle in the center of the kitchen.

"Mmmom, Mommy," I whimper.

"Can you tell me what's wrong? Here, sit down."

I sit down heavily and in a tiny voice I say it, "Mom. I'm pregnant."

I'm not sure she's heard me.

"Mom?" I say once more.

I don't know what else to say. She's supposed to say something. Say *anything*. Just don't hate me, Mom. Please don't hate me.

"Are you sure?" she asks slowly.

"I took a home pregnancy test by myself, and it read positive."

"Oh, my baby, I'm sorry." Her eyes cloud up and her lips press together, trembling.

"No, *I'm* sorry, Mom. I'm so, *so* sorry. Can you ever forgive me? I just feel so worthless. You must be so ashamed of me. I mean, what will all your friends think?"

She puts her arms around me and draws me close. Her face is against my hair. Her breath feels warm and comfortable on my neck. Her arms tighten around me, and for the first time since I realized I was pregnant I feel, what is it . . . good? No, not good. Just not alone. Like it's OK even though it's not OK.

"It's not important what people think, honey," she whispers. "I still love you. Daddy and I both love you. You're still our little girl." This makes her cry even harder. "We'll have to have you see a doctor. Do you know how many months you are?"

"Just about two, I guess." I wait for her to ask who the father is. I wonder if this will change things. I want it to stay like this, just us girls here without any scolding or preaching. Just comfort.

"Who's the . . . father?" she asks.

"Umm, Keeler, Jim's friend. I told him this afternoon. He wants me to get an abortion."

Mom sighs and doesn't answer. Her eyes are locked and very faraway. My secret had infected so many people in just a matter of hours. It wasn't my secret anymore. It touched everyone.

"Will God punish me, I mean, my baby could die, or I could die."

"You mean if you had an abortion?"

"No, Mom. I know I couldn't go through with an abortion. I just couldn't live with the guilt of taking a life or the what-if's afterwards. But I'm scared. Do you think God will punish me?"

"God knows you're sorry, honey. I think the agony you must've already gone through is punishment enough. God is a loving Father, sweetheart." Mom gets up and pours me some cider. Things seem to be settling down a little, like I can breathe easier.

"Will you tell Dad for me? I don't think I can do it. It's embarrassing, Mom."

"Well, you better get used to it now, because you won't be able to hide how you look." She sighs. I wonder what she's really thinking.

I go up to my room to sleep without dinner. I've had enough for one day. All the unanswered decisions don't have to be made tonight. Mom understands. She has surprised me by being so forgiving. Maybe one day I'll know what it feels like to love something that is a part of me.

I sit by my window in my window seat. A plane passes through some clouds like an invisible needle and emerges again, pulsing a tiny light. And under the street lamp I think I see light snow falling. Yes, it's definitely snowing the first snow of the year. And the snow covers everything.

CHAPTER

23

Jim

Like all good things come to an end. Then . . . then what? What's left is you.

I'm out of grass and it isn't quite the weekend. I'm supposed to meet Keeler tonight at the Red Rooster. Lately all we do is get together and get toasted. We rarely ever do anything without getting intoxicated first. Right now I'm crashing. I have an intense desire to curl up on the couch in the lobby of this office and die for several hours. Which is what I do.

I awake to the sound of a buzzer. Buzz! Buzz! Buzz! Buzzzz! I am not convinced yet that the buzz isn't from inside my brain. I leap off the couch and dash through the office, hunting desperately for the source of the buzz. Then I hear a pinched voice through the intercom system. "Jim! I'm at the front door, you spazz! It's Holly." I have no idea why Holly has hunted me down, and I'm not that thrilled about being aroused from my slumber.

I unlock five billion locks and combinations before letting her in. "How did you know I was here?" I ask. "You look terrible."

"Thanks a lot. I saw your car outside, and I remembered you clean here at night," she says, breathlessly. She really does look bad. She has that pale, worried look I sort of remember.

"Jim, I have to tell you something. Maybe it's not me that should tell you, or it's none of my business. I don't know."

"Just chill and tell me," I say, a little annoyed. Holly used to pull this stuff on me when we were still going out. It was her way to get attention. She called it "getting hyper." She's serious enough now, though, almost ready to cry, I think.

"It's Sonia. Jim, she's pregnant. I just saw her at the mall. She's a wreck, and I was the perfect wench to her. I just didn't know what to say," she rambles. "I feel bad I was so judgmental. I don't think I was much of a help."

I gasp and stagger backward. "Wait. My sister's pregnant? As in baby?"

Holly nods and puts her face in her hands, starting to bawl.

"Just tell me who did it," I explode. "But I think I already know."

Holly can barely speak. I can tell she's trying to go easy on me and at the same time she's pretty torn up herself.

"It's Keeler, Jim," she wails.

Right then I wonder, if it were any other guy in the world, would I want to kill him this badly? Is it that someone hurt my sister, or is it that the someone just happened to be Keeler, my new friend? Yeah, it would have to be him. That's the way it goes for me.

"Jim, are you going to be OK? I mean, I know this news is a major shock for you, but, uh, you and Sonia haven't really been that close lately. I'm sort of surprised that you care at all," Holly says.

"Well, guess what? I'm surprised too. I'm surprised I have even an ounce of compassion in me. I've treated Sonia really rotten lately, and now I guess it's time to wake up—show her what a brother should be."

I'm not quite sure what I might do, but many violent things come to mind. I don't take much time to think about it, I just leave. I have never felt anger in my muscles before. It's not even close to the pumping up and killer tactics we used in football. This is the real thing.

I drive like a mad dog to the restaurant. I hope Keeler is there so that I don't waste any of this wrath on anyone else's face. He's not there yet, so I pace around back behind the restaurant, back by the dumpsters and trash. I don't know how anyone could be low enough to take advantage of my little sister. There is this acute pain in my gut. It's not even for Sonia, really; it's just this angry hurt at Keeler for being like everyone's said; anger at whatever it is that makes us play dirty; anger at, well, just that I can't do anything about this situation . . . except punish it somehow.

Keeler's car screeches up to where I am

anxiously kicking at boxes and storming around trying to keep warm. I'm not sure if I'm cold or just shaking because I'm mad. Keeler steps halfway out of the car when I grab him by his collar and throw him back against the car.

"You scum!" I yell.

"Whoa, man . . . what's . . . goin' . . . on?" he sputters. "Wait a minute!"

"My sister's pregnant, and you're the father! That's what's goin' on," I say. Not giving him any chance to defend himself, I'm completely overcome with rage. I throw some punches at him, pound blindly at nowhere in particular.

"Take it easy, man. You're out of control," Keeler yells.

"You didn't have the courage to tell me. Don't talk to me about control." I throw out my words to sting him.

It's almost like I'm wrestling myself, beating out all the despicable lies and games I've played the last few months, the hard and hateful attitude I've had toward my parents. I take it out on Keeler. With every punch I grow more violent until he turns the fight around and pins my arm, the one attached to my bad shoulder, behind my back. He holds me at my weak spot and I can't move. Not satisfied, he slams me to the ground, my arm still twisted behind me.

"I hate your guts, man!" I grumble. He stands over me looking like he might give me one last kick to finish me off.

He doesn't say anything but jumps in his car and squeals off. I must've cut my cheek when I fell in the gravel. I wipe a smear of blood from my face and try to get up. Blood has always freaked me out. I'm still stunned and surprised by my own capacity to hate so intensely. Like I could possibly kill someone.

So many scenes swim around in my mixed-up head. Back where it all started when I introduced Keeler to Sonia . . . Sonia, who has always been just my stupid sister, who I never talk to anymore, who I guess I must not know very well. And, I'm the one responsible. She can thank me for being the worst example of a brother, a loser, this jerk flailing around without any standards to keep. I can see me the time I tried my first joint . . . there I go, deeper and deeper into destruction without much of a second thought.

There's that little lump in my coat pocket. I pull out the cellophane bag and without much regret toss the pot into the nearby dumpster. Into oblivion. Squandered money. One last escape from facing the facts about who I've become. I get in the car and drive away from the scene. Shake it off. You're OK. You're OK. Just drive until you figure it all out. Put it together.

I find I have driven myself straight to the stadium, which is lighted up like a billboard: "Welcome Home." Funny how I can come here and feel almost peaceful inside. This is where the old Jim lives. I climb the bleachers to the very top to admire the view. I think of the yardage I used to skim with ease, and run and run, full of life, like I could knock down anything.

I sit here hunched over on the bleachers full of heaviness, and I feel incredibly small. I'm alone in my stadium. I start to think of how I was watched and cheered by so many people. They saw everything from up here—my fumbles, my successes. And people watch me now. Whether I like to think so or not, who I am for God does matter. How I handle what is thrown at me. Do I run, or do I trip and slide?

Right now I want more than anything for God to hear me. I shout out, "Hey!" into the wide mouth of the stadium. My own voice answers me and disappears. I don't know where to begin with a prayer. "I've been running away from You" is all that comes in a whisper.

The bleachers echo and shake with the steps of someone behind me. At the top I see Coach, who has spotted me. I feel like I've been caught trespassing.

"Coach, hi, I saw the lights on . . ."

"Yeah, we've got a couple burned out. Were you looking for me?"

"N-n-no, I just needed to see the field." I try to flick off the cigarette I'm holding and turn my head away so that he doesn't notice the cut on my face. He plunks down beside me like a long-lost friend.

"How've you been? Are you doin' all right?" he asks kindly.

"Yeah, I mean, I dunno. This year's really turning out to be a crummy one. There's a lot of stuff I just don't understand."

"Do you feel like talking about it?"

Suddenly I want to tell this man everything. I don't care if I've thought he was a geek; I can see that he still cares. I still haven't managed to extinguish my cigarette, but that doesn't seem to bother him.

"I've just been into some really stupid things lately. I feel like I've really blown it. And now my sister's, uh, in trouble . . . Coach, why does God allow stuff like this?" I blurt.

"I hope I'm not sounding trite, but you know, sometimes God uses some heavy things to wake us up, to shake us so that we turn to Him like He wants us to. Too bad it takes some pretty tragic things to get us to realize where we've strayed and that we desperately need Him."

"I don't know why we can't choose to please Him on our own . . . like it's not always cool to follow Him. I want to want to please Him. Right now I guess I'm so sick of the way I've been living I just want to give in and give all those things up, but who knows if I'll feel that way tomorrow? You can think you're strong and still choose the wrong path. How do you decide?"

"God doesn't want us to go about it alone. He gives us the direction, if we ask Him. He'll give you the courage to make the right decisions if you listen to Him."

"I've kind of forgotten about stuff like this. It seems like I've heard it all my life—it's just never been that real to me," I say.

Coach mentions the opportunity to be on track yet this year. I throw down my cigarette and squash it out. I never thought of this, either, but the way Coach is being to me, almost forgiving me, is probably how God's grace is. He like, gives you another chance. Even though He totally knows what you've done and everything, He still accepts you and gives you a shove to keep you in the game.

Another night I'm sitting Indian style in front of the TV in our family room. So far I have managed to stay out of the firing line that is just up the stairs in the kitchen. From where I sit I can catch pieces of urgent explanations and even more urgent questioning. I wish I could spare Sonia from the pain of decision. Mom and Dad can be almost relentless sometimes.

On the TV Mrs. Brady ruffles her son's hair playfully, warning him not to call his sister a stinker ever again. Funny how the conflicts in the Brady family appear to be so refreshing compared to how intense real life's shockers are. Me and Sonia used to watch these shows religiously every day after school. We'd sit down here with our after-school snacks and digest these happy plots of TV life like they were the definition on reality. Same with our favorite cartoons. No matter how high the cliff Wile E. Coyote was pushed from, his fall was always shaken off. The explosives turned his fur to soot for a moment, and then he was off and running again. Danger was funny because you knew these characters never got seriously hurt.

Sonia comes down the stairs and stands quietly behind the couch, drawn in at once to the story on the television. She watches transfixed there, almost as if I should ignore her red face and swollen eyes. Like this is just a typical night and nothing's wrong.

"Which one is this?" she asks. Her voice sounds pinched and strange. I'm almost relieved to talk about TV shows, though. Maybe it can postpone the more serious things I feel pressured to say.

"This is the one where Cindy blames Bobby for stealing her doll, Kitty Carryall, when it was really Tiger the dog who stole it," I say automatically.

"They find the doll in the doghouse, right?"

"Yeah. I don't like them when they're little like this. Cindy's just too cute, and look at Bobby. What a little dork."

"That's how you looked in first grade. You wore your little pointy-collared shirts with the top button buttoned way up to your neck," Sonia laughs.

"I remember how I insisted on wearing that macrame necklace I made in Girl Scouts for my third-grade picture. What a big deal that was."

A commercial comes on for a candy that's supposed to be more fun than just any candy, and I am suddenly forced to fill in the space between us. Sonia is sitting on the couch now with her arms folded across her stomach. I blink hard, trying not to think about her a few months from now, big as a house, with a smock on. Not Sonia. Not little Sonia.

"I don't think we've watched TV down here like this for a million years. So how are you feeling, anyway?" I ask.

"I'll make it. I guess you heard it was Keeler, huh?" she asks shyly.

"Well, yeah, I did. I'm sorry about—everything. I should have warned you about Keeler."

"That wouldn't have made any difference. I liked Keeler from the beginning. I made the choice on my own. It's no one's fault but mine."

"Yeah, but I could've kept you from getting hurt. Keeler's the kind of guy who'll do anything that seems fun at the moment. He doesn't think of what it will cost; he just does it."

"That doesn't matter, Jim. I can't blame others for my temporary blindness. It all comes down to me and God in the end, you know?"

"I just can't forgive myself for the rotten example I've been for you. I've been into some pretty stupid things lately myself. What a loser. I've already asked God's forgiveness for turning my back on Him, but do you . . ."

"What, Jim?" Sonia asks.

I look at her there, her face bare and young, tear-streaked. She's such a tender heart, not trying to defend herself, really.

"I just hope you can forgive me for pushing you away, for almost wishing that you'd make a mistake and get in trouble for it—I can't believe how lousy that is to wish on someone!" Sonia slides down off the couch to where I am, ready to cry but trying to be the big guy.

"It's going to be OK. We're friends. Look, we're actually talking and we're watching reruns on TV."

Then she does something I had completely forgotten about, a game we used to play. She pinches my arm hard and twists it, then jumps back so I won't get her worse.

"Gottcha!" she grins.

Keeler

I have consumed an entire box of powdered sugar donuts. Munchies in a big way. Fornication flashbacks. I have killed many brain cells. Think. Think. Dang. Can't even have a neat fling anymore.

Now I remember why I got so messed up last night. That heavy confrontation at the mall with Sonia. Fumbling idiot. "Guess what? You're a dad." Ta-da! Yeah, and then Jim beating the living snot out of me. Man, I'm glad I bailed out of that one fast enough. He was nuts.

I'm in my cocoon, my car, and I'm not coming out until the stink of my rotting body bothers the neighbors or until Jack and Judy miss me. Gee, which will come first? I fall asleep to some macabre group angsting out, singing death-wish songs. It could be a school day. I'm not sure.

Sincerely, I do feel bad for Sonia. But really,

I can only say two things: One, I knew better. And two: Be more careful next time. I must be dozing. I peer bleary-eyed from underneath some blankets that permanently reside in this car. The world is a bright familiar glare through the frosty glass. I suppose it's snowing.

I've been quite a tough cowboy. I deserve a badge for existing like I do. I'm serious. Every human being should be able to hold down at least one person they can call their friend, and I've blown it.

God, if there is a God who can defend me, knows that I made an honest effort to tell Jim that one day in his office. I tried to tell him about me and Sonia and that I was sort of a father. I actually wanted his advice then. I wanted him to help me find the boundaries. Because if I recall, there are boundaries in this life. I've been taught to live by them since day one, but unfortunately I've chosen to forget what those guidelines actually are.

Snow falls more heavily now. I can't see out of my chamber. A horrible thought comes to me. Will I suffocate here? If I turn the engine on, will the fumes become trapped under all of that cotton? It would be so simple to do. Annihilate. All I want is peace. I want peace. I want to be in a place where I don't have to think about things. Non-existence. Me being dead. Would that be it? I mean, after the putting to sleep, do I go to hell or—well, it certainly wouldn't be heaven at this point. If I'm going to do this I better hit it now—but how about if I just believe there's nothing after life? Whoa, that's too radical. Nothing. Non-being. Maybe if I knew I was headed for heaven I wouldn't be too scared to go through with it.

I lay my head down for another timeless moment. All of a sudden there is this scraping on my window. I jump up, hitting my head on the roof. Someone is pounding on the window. Caught for possession! Confiscation! I'm not getting out. They'll have to dig me out.

"Keeler, Keeler, are you in there? Hey, Keeler, are you in there?

The voice was familiar. It was Jim's. He had returned for his final vengeance. I rolled down the window, causing walls of snow to slide like an avalanche off of the car.

"What are you doing, Keeler?" he asks calmly.

"Well, I thought I'd order out, and then wait in here until I freeze to death." I am almost serious. Warped, really warped.

"Do you want to go somewhere to warm up? You look blue." He pauses. "OK, I know you probably don't want to see me, but you sort of missed the debate today, and I thought you might be in trouble or sick or something."

"Oh, man. The debate. So how did us free-will people come out?" I laugh.

"Well, I didn't do so hot by myself, but Holly had some good things to say," he began.

"Save it, OK?" I'm sure Jim plows through the snowbanks just to tell me our lives are determined. "Sorry about the debate," I mumble.

"Look, Keeler, I don't expect you to be thrilled to see me after the fight I started. A lot of heavy things have happened in the last twenty-four hours, but I'm sorry for the fight. And I don't hate you, man."

"That's cool, man. Hey, what can I say? I'm real sorry for your sister . . . and uh . . ." I can't believe he's apologizing. I invite him into the car, though I can't think of what to say next. I hand him a powdered donut, which he accepts. A peace offering, maybe. A little gracias for, well, for saving my life.

"Why are you out here in your car, you mad-man?" Jim laughs.

"Because I live here."

"You—what? You don't really live in your car . . . do you?"

"Yep, this is where you end up when you've done everything the wrong way. But the main thing is, man, I've done it the way I wanted to. I've been in control." I say it, yet I don't believe my own philosophy anymore. Jim is in disbelief, I can tell. He looks like he's about to tell me something really important.

"So how are your supplies holding out?" I ask, changing the subject.

"Well, it's like this . . . I threw them out," he smirks proudly.

"Wait. Why did I already know that? You squirrel. You're all right, you know that?" I look at him and start to laugh. He wears a perfect beard of powdered sugar. And I'm straight when I tell you that. For real.